Dig Two Graves

HEND SALAH

A HellBound Books LLC Publication

www.hellboundbookspublishing.com

Dedication

For my family, without whom this would have been impossible.

Hend Salah

Dig Two Graves

<u>ONE</u>

She was sitting on a cold concrete floor, gagged, bound, and blinded. Nothing but a stale silence encompassed her. A putrid smell emanated from something to her left, sending her into a fit of coughs. It was so strong that she could almost taste it. It filled her mouth and nose, feeding her senses a disgusting smell created by something—or someone—that had been left alone to rot. She imagined a corpse sprawled just beyond her feet: its face having decayed so intensely that facial features were no longer visible; wounds festering soundlessly as insects found refuge inside them; skin hanging off its feet and toes with mutilated nails; skull crushed almost entirely, neither discernible as male nor female.

She fidgeted and fought with the ropes that bound her, but only managed enough movement to fall onto her left side. Instead of meeting dry concrete, her face was submerged in a thick liquid that harbored a smell that was as fragrant as dead flowers on a fresh grave. She closed her eyes to keep them from being irritated by it.

The liquid seeped into her mouth from the corner of

her lips, but so sickening was the taste that her stomach immediately heaved. Vomit erupted from her mouth, leaving a pool of her own bile to become an addition to the substance she had already been battling. Her disgust intensified, sending another upheaval from her stomach to grace the floor.

A door was dragged open, and she heard voices of two men. She didn't understand the language, but they sounded cheerful. A moment later, they began to laugh, and she assumed that they had caught sight of her current predicament. Their guffaws echoed off the walls as her body heaved once again, this time failing to project anything new. There was no longer anything inside her to throw up.

Someone grabbed her hair and dragged her out of the room. She screamed, but the shrill sound only intensified their amusement. She was pulled roughly down a corridor with a harsh, uneven concrete floor. Cracks and small rocks passed under her, tearing her clothes and spilling her blood. Deep cuts formed lines down her back and arms, the red liquid soaking what was left of her shirt.

The person came to a sudden halt and dropped her hair. Her head slammed against the floor and her vision blurred momentarily. She heard an animal-like snarl, and then was once again dragged by her hair across the floor. She was pushed into another room, this one less odorous, and her blindfold was lifted. The only source of light was a lit torch upon a wall that only illuminated enough of her surroundings for her eyes to catch distinct outlines. The figures that had moved her were nothing more than shadows in the dark. She only had a few seconds to commit their forms to memory before they left the room, slamming the wooden door behind them.

She turned her head to look around the room. The entire area was bare, save for one steel table and a metal something to sit on that looked nothing like an actual chair. The room was small and simple: four walls, one source of light, and a wooden door. Even in the midst of the pain, it interested her that the door was so easily penetrable. If it were so safe here, why had the other door been so heavy and difficult to open? She assumed that she had been alone there, as well.

A moment later, two more figures were dragged in. One of them was completely lifeless, and the other's blindfold was not lifted. The latter simply lay there, whimpering and shaking incessantly, while the other was unconscious. Again, the men closed the door and left.

She didn't dare speak. A man and a small creature entered the room. She examined the thing as closely as she was able to under the ineffective lighting. It had four talons and one wing, making it almost birdlike in a sense, but it had no beak, and the wing seemed to be made of leather rather than feathers. She tried to turn her head to see more, but she couldn't move.

They still spoke in a tongue she did not recognize, and she made no attempt to say a word to them. She had never been easy to silence, but she had also never been thick. She just lay on the cold floor, still bleeding, watching the creature come close to the woman whose body was trembling next to her.

The creature reached one talon to her chest and plunged it into her flesh. The woman screamed, but the thing wasn't perturbed. It slowly cut a straight line that ended just above her navel. Blood spurted out of the wound and the woman lost consciousness. The creature lapped up the blood quickly, not losing a single drop to the floor. Minutes passed, and finally, it was done. It turned to her.

Her heart pounded in her chest as it approached, but not one sound escaped her. As it drew closer, she *saw its face more clearly. It had beady black eyes and holes for a nose. Where its mouth should have been was a crooked line. It had no lips, and she didn't understand how it had been drinking the other woman's blood so easily—until it opened its mouth.*

The crooked line snapped open. So wide was the opening that it stretched between the area where a nose should have been and its pointed, dirt encrusted chin. It exposed sharp, glistening white teeth that more closely resembled a closed steel trap than actual teeth. Each triangular incisor fit cleanly with the next, leaving no gap or hole between them.

She braced herself as it reached its talon over her, just as it had done to the lifeless body lying next to her and dug it into her chest. She didn't react or whimper. She didn't scream or beg. She kept her eyes on its grotesque face and resolutely kept herself from making a sound, her expression displaying a hair of defiance.

It seemed surprised. It wrenched its talon out of her body harshly, and her blood spilled over. Still, she just watched it, refusing to give it the satisfaction of knowing how much pain it was inflicting on her. It turned to the other figure in the room. It squawked something at them and left. The thing turned to her again and—

Jezebel woke with a jolt and found herself still sitting in the chair by her bed. She had broken out into a cold sweat; a common occurrence when she was locked inside the darkest, most self-deprecating corners of her vastly overburdened mind. She stood and looked around her. Her oversized, circular bed was made, the floor was void of unidentified objects or clothes, and everything was in the exact spot that it was supposed to be in. Not one hair was out of place. It was unnerving; she had always been uncomfortable with perfection.

Everything in the room was extravagant to obscene

degrees. It was excessively large, her closet alone nearly rivaling that of a queen who did not wear the same thing twice. The white walls were decorated by expensive paintings, and the carpet was a lavish plush that met her bare feet with warm welcome. The entirety of her ceiling was covered with a spotless mirror. She had purchased the house that way, and though it was a nuisance to wake up to the sight of her own face every day, she had never made an effort to make a change.

She had fallen asleep fully clothed; the black pantsuit she had donned the previous morning was no longer as sharp as it had been when she put it on. Her back ached from the awkwardness of her position. The chair was uncomfortable and not at all fit for sleeping. The leather was always cold, no matter the temperature of the room or how long she had been sitting on it. It was the unwelcome kind of cold that offered no consolation on even the hottest of days.

She vacated the chair and went to the bathroom just as Hanem ran up the stairs with chaotically stacked papers in hand. She turned to him and waited. The middle-aged—unnaturally pale for someone of Korean descent—man stopped in front of her and gasped for breath. Hanem lacked any real physical strength. However, his mind was sharper than most, and his temper was cunningly controlled. He was calm in nature, but when pushed into a position of anger where he knew there would be no consequences for his actions, he became a shadow of who he seemed to be. It was rare when this anger could cause physical damage, but he had an intelligence that was far more useful to him than his almost worthless build.

When he finally pulled himself together, he said, "There are six evaluations waiting for you, and one of them is already sitting in your office, tapping her foot impatiently."

"I don't hurry for anyone."

"I think you might want to make an exception, today."

"Why?"

"You'll enjoy it."

"I hate when you're cryptic."

"I know, but I like when you are confused."

He ran back down the stairs before she responded, wielding the same papers he had brought unexplained. He was so often in a frenzy that he over-exerted himself. It was unhealthy, but he took care of himself well enough.

She took a short shower and then walked into her room quickly. Although she lived alone, she was uncomfortable being outside of the bedroom or bathroom without being fully clothed. She pulled random articles of clothing out of her closet, not really seeing them, and then tossed them onto the bed, not bothering to be careful or neat.

She chose a skirted suit she had never worn before. She rarely wore the same thing twice, not for vanity, but because she donated her wardrobe to various organizations. She was not the most philanthropic of the rich, but she believed that old and tattered clothes were meant for the garbage, not the less fortunate.

The black skirt she wore fell past her knees, and a short slit up the right side revealed that the other side of the fabric was a crimson color—the exact shade of the blouse that was tucked into it. She wore a black blazer that was only slightly shorter than the length of her upper body and black pumps for shoes, the bottom of which were also a matching shade of red.

She turned to the mirror and quickly dried her brown hair. She brushed it thoroughly before putting it into a neat bun. She surveyed herself for a few moments and then turned to leave for work. There would surely be multiple clients waiting, but she rarely spared a moment to think about how long they had been there—or how any of them were actually doing. Most of them deserved to sit uncomfortably until she decided to take the time to see them. Almost all of them were criminals in one way or another. They had been forced by a judge to come see her.

Her practice was just across the street from her home, which eliminated any need for her to drive. She had never minded the extra effort, as she never exercised otherwise. Today, however, she wasn't feeling up to the walk. She walked out of her bedroom and went down the circular flight of stairs. They were made with black marble, and wound from the third level of the manor to the foyer. The top of the stairs led into a vast living room, and marble barring lined what was essentially a hole in the floor. Anyone who fell over the bars would likely meet an embarrassing death.

The bottom level of the house itself was an optical illusion that could dizzy anyone looking at it from above. There were black and white pinwheels that appeared to be spinning slowly. Staring for long periods of time could easily cause a migraine, or at least momentary confusion. It was a small, and sometimes effective, defensive mechanism that she used on people she happened to dislike by simply asking them to look down. The man who had created the thing had been its first victim by leaning too far over the balcony to see his final masterpiece one time too many. He had told her several times that he wondered whether it would kill him if he fell onto it from such great heights. Now, he knew the answer.

She left through the glass-stained front door and stepped into her double-ended driveway. Several cars were parked neatly in line around a large fountain that resembled a rushing waterfall. Its white stone lit up as soon as the sun went down, and around the outskirts of the fountain were beds of white and red roses, thorns very much intact. She had not chosen the fountain herself, but the original flowers were terrible lilac shrubs that were far too bright. They could only be aesthetically pleasing to people who needed sedatives for some kind of deluded euphoria.

She stepped into the back seat of a black car that she assumed was expensive. She hadn't chosen it herself. The man behind the steering wheel pulled out of the driveway and drove through the empty pathway that led to her office. Her estate was extremely large, and she had chosen to practice on her own grounds for security reasons. She liked to be able to see everything that belonged to her from just one window inside the manor. It was safer that way.

Hanem saw her through the window and sent in the first client, who was an impatient woman wearing more make-up than necessary. Her hair was dyed a fake shade of blonde that was almost white, but she lacked the judgment to match her eyebrows to make it realistic. She was very tall, slightly overweight, and had large brown doe eyes. She may have been pretty had she not been wearing a repulsively sour expression on her face.

"You kept me waiting!" she said.

Jezebel's tone was extremely cold as she said, "Sit down."

The girl sat. "I just need you to sign my paper that says that I don't have any anger problems, because I do *not*."

Jezebel opened the file and observed it. The girl's name was Linda Baker. She had been arrested five times for public disturbance, three times for public indecency, twice for assaulting four police officers, and her latest charge was aggravated assault against her father using a knife and a steel pipe. The reason listed was financial disagreement.

"Tell me about your first few arrests. How old were you?"

"I'm not here for your stupid therapy. Sign the paper."

"No."

The girl stood. "Then I'll just go to someone else."

"You can."

The girl stalked toward the door, but before she could open it, Jezebel said, "But I wouldn't leave this room if I were you."

The girl turned back. "And why is that?"

"Because as soon as you step foot out of that door, I will make a call to the judge who presided over your case. I'll tell him all about the fit that you threw just now and recommend that you're committed to an inpatient psychiatric unit for a complete evaluation."

"You wouldn't."

"If you believe I'm bluffing, go ahead and leave."

The girl made a noise that Jezebel had never heard a human being make, and then grudgingly threw herself back into the chair she had just vacated. She crossed her arms and glared at Jezebel.

"Answer my question," Jezebel said.

"The public indecency charges happened when I was in high school. I was just a teenager, okay?"

"And how old are you, now?"

"It's right in front of you."

"How old are you now?"

"Twenty-two."

"What about the altercations with the first two police officers?"

"They kept telling me not to jaywalk, like that's a real thing!"

"It is a real thing."

"Well, I did not know that."

"And the second?"

"They kept looking down my shirt."

"It says here that you were severely intoxicated and were attempting to deface their car."

"I don't remember."

"You were also underage."

"So? Everyone was drinking."

"Unfortunately, only you were caught."

"That doesn't mean I'm the only devil."

"But you're the only devil on trial."

"What the hell are you saying?"

"I am saying," Jezebel said and closed the file. "You have no anger management problems."

"I already told you that!"

"You do, however, deserve far more than six months of anger management, and I suspect that a light punishment such as this was allowed because of exceptions made due to your financial or social status."

"That's none of your business!"

"You want me to sign this?"

"Yes!"

"Then you will sit outside this door and write two hundred and fifty words telling me in great detail exactly why I shouldn't call the District Attorney's office and recommend that you are given at least six months in jail."

"What!"

"And you can consider that an act of kindness from me. I'm feeling charitable, today."

"I won't do it!"

"Twenty minutes is all I am giving you. The decision is yours to make. Get out."

The girl walked out, and Jezebel sat back in her chair. She reveled in the victory for a few moments, and then Hanem sent in another person. This time, it was a girl Jezebel saw regularly. She was only fifteen, but she looked no less than eighteen, and she was beautiful. Her name was Nadine. She was cursed with a rat's nest of problems that Jezebel had made less progress with in six months than she made in two with any other client.

Though truly helping people through mental or behavioral problems was less than secondary on the list of things she actually wanted to do, she spent some real effort on a few of her regular patients. This girl in particular was one that Jezebel truly gave her full attention, largely because she had a childlike innocence about her that Jezebel rarely saw in people.

The girl sat down and smiled.

"You look happy," Nadine said.

"I see your embellishment problem still hasn't subsided."

"Well, you never tell me not to."

"And we're lying, again?"

"You're being abrasive."

"Define abrasive."

"Jezebel White."

"You're witty, today."

"It's nothing that's not true."

"I am what I am."

"And I say what I say."

"Funny."

"Side-splittingly funny?"

"We're directing the conversation away from me, now."

"You're no fun."

"That shouldn't be news to you."

"Back to talking about my horrible life, then?"

"Yes."

In the middle of the session, the Baker girl charged in. She pushed the door so hard that it slammed into the white wall behind it harshly. Both Nadine and Jezebel jumped and looked at her, both of their expressions melting into extreme agitation when they recognized the perpetrator.

The girl slammed the paper on Jezebel's desk and crossed her arms. "Now, sign my paper."

Jezebel put the pen and notepad that she had been holding down and folded her hands on her desk.

"Because you finished so quickly, I will not sign this."

"WHAT? YOU SAID YOU WOULD!"

"Calm down or you will leave."

"You said you would sign, you bitch!"

"Don't talk to her like that!" Nadine yelled.

"Quiet, Nadine," Jezebel snapped.

"Sorry."

Jezebel looked at the obnoxious creature standing before her. "You are sorely mistaken if you think my signature will help you."

"Of course it will!"

"No. If I sign this paper, then you will lose your anger management plea and likely be sentenced to a reasonable amount of jail-time or a high—and well-deserved—amount of community service hours. If I do not sign and say that you do have an anger problem, you will only attend an anger management class every week for six to eight months. You can decide your own fate, if you want. I won't play deity with your future, Miss Baker."

"That can't be true."

"If you had half a brain, you would realize that it is."

"Don't talk down to me."

"I'll do what I want."

"Will you promise that I won't go to jail?"

"No."

The girl faltered. "Okay. Don't sign."

"Goodbye."

She left and slammed the door behind her. Jezebel leaned back in her chair feeling satisfied with herself. She had a deep hatred for children who were born to affluent families and viewed the world as their personal playground. Nothing and no one mattered to them. Someone, somewhere, had to put them in their place; preferably in a way that would be at least a tad bit painful. There was nothing sadistic about that, but even if it were, justice sometimes was.

The door opened a crack, and Hanem stuck his balding head through the door and raised his thin eyebrows.

"Well?" he asked.

"Save me the trouble of remembering that one."

Hanem grinned. "With pleasure."

"You can go."

"I was right."

"Get out, Hanem."

"It won't kill you to admit that I was right."

"It might."

He pulled away and closed the door. Jezebel turned back to check in with the girl in front of her. Nadine's arms were crossed, and she was sitting back in her chair with a smirk on her face.

"You look amused," Jezebel said.

"That was terrifying."

"You don't look scared."

"You would never hurt me."

"Why so sure?"

"I am your favorite patient."

Jezebel laughed. "If you say so."

"You can be so intimidating sometimes," she said.

"It's one of my stronger suits, I think."

"And the most attractive."

"Are you flirting with me, Nadine?"

"You aren't allowed to date your patients."

"Or girls under eighteen."

"Otherwise…"

"No."

"Rats."

TWO

Night fell, and Jezebel gathered the day's files to look over them one last time. She had seen eight clients, seven of them female and one of them male. She tossed away his file and looked into the others. She made notes and observations to look at again later. Her handwriting was small and barely legible, making it very difficult for someone who was not accustomed to her penmanship to read it.

Just as she opened Nadine's, Hanem rushed in. His eyebrows were furrowed, and his mouth was pursed in a way that she had learned was his way of displaying his irritation. He closed the door tightly behind him and walked around her desk.

She leaned away. "What are you doing?"

"A detective named Asher Wilson is here to see you," he said.

"We're closed."

"He refuses to take that as an answer."

"Why are you whispering?"

"He's a homicide detective."

"What?"

The door opened, and a tall, fairly built man entered the room. The sleeves of his black collared shirt were rolled up to his elbows, and three buttons were undone. He was wearing a smirk that created a dimple in his right cheek that may have been charming had it been on someone less unwelcome. He leaned on her desk with both hands, coming too close to her for it to be appropriate.

"I told your secretary here not to keep me waiting," he said.

"You have no authority over either of us," she said. "You're standing too close to me."

He moved back. "It's important."

"I don't care."

"Just a moment of your time."

"We are closed," Jezebel repeated.

"To patients," he said. "Since you're still here, I thought I might pop in. I chose this time so I wouldn't disturb your work."

"You're still disturbing me."

"Not intentionally."

"Please don't take this to be rude, but what do you want?"

"I don't see how that could possibly not be rude."

"Get out."

"Don't like officers of the law?"

"Particularly not when they are so intrusive."

"Just a few questions from the police department, if that's alright with you, Dr. White," said Wilson, the light dancing in his bright blue eyes betraying his attempt at sounding stern. He knew just how irritating he was and he was deeply enjoying it.

"Miss White," she said.

"I'm sorry. I was under the impression that you hold a doctoral degree. From Yale, no less."

"Are you stalking me?"

"Not well, obviously."

"I do hold a doctoral degree, but that isn't any of your business. Again, is there something I can help you with?"

"I'm just wondering if you've been paying attention to the news, lately."

"Depends on the part you're referring to."

"I'm sure you can figure out of what part a homicide detective would be referring to."

"You assume that I know who you are?"

"Are you accustomed to having police officers come talk to you about petty theft?"

"I'm not accustomed to being interrogated by police officers at all, especially not on my own property."

"I'm only looking for an answer to my question."

"You'll find that you haven't asked one yet."

"Have you heard of the recent disappearance of a young woman named Athena Elias?"

"Something about it, yes. Why?"

"Do you also know of two other girls of about the same age who have also gone missing, recently?"

"The few details I've committed to memory. Again, why?"

"You don't know them?"

"Miss Elias, I've met once. The others, I can't say I have."

"In what capacity did you know Elias?"

"As far as I remember, she has been in for an evaluation. Came once and then never again."

"But not the other two."

"You're baiting me."

"I don't mean to."

"What are you getting at?"

"I'm only expressing interest in the fact that you claim to not know the other two, when all three have been patients in your office."

"I claim."

"Answer the question, Miss White."

"I could report you for interrogating me like this, Detective."

"I know."

"I can't remember every person who comes in for a simple evaluation. If you would like to check my records, I have a great number of these cases passing through my office every single day."

"I'm finding it hard to ignore the only connection these victims have to each other."

"I don't care. You've overstayed your welcome."

He paused for a moment and looked down at her desk. He lifted the book that she had left open a few nights before. "The Faerie Queene."

"Put that down."

He thumbed through the pages. "I've never heard of this book."

"Don't touch anything that doesn't belong to you. You're walking on very thin ice as it is."

He looked up and set his intense eyes on Jezebel. "It doesn't look very interesting."

She got up and snatched it out of his hand. "This is one of the most complex, breathtakingly beautiful, sensibly mad pieces of unfinished work you can ever hope to set your hands on. Get the hell out of my office. That is not a request."

"But I have another question."

"And I have no interest in hearing it."

"Why did the court choose you to do these evaluations?"

"You can ask the judge."

"I am asking you."

"I owe you no explanations."

"Is it because your work is better than others, or might there be other, maybe illicit, reasons involved?"

"You'll make your own assumptions no matter what I say."

"I'd still like to hear your side."

"You can't always get what you want."

He didn't relent. "Do you use a different technique than everyone else? I doubt that yours is better."

"Stay out of it, Dodo."

"Excuse me?"

"I'm tired of asking you to leave."

He ignored her and looked around the room. He stopped at the sight of the framed diplomas on the wall. He walked over to them and picked her graduate school diploma off the wall.

"Fancy school," he said.

"If you say so, then it must be true."

"Jezebel is a special name."

"I didn't choose it."

"Don't like it?"

"You have three seconds to get the hell off my property before I make a phone call you will regret."

"Fine. Goodnight."

He put the diploma back on the wall, and then turned and left without another word. She went to her window to watch him. It had started raining. He walked out of the practice and ran over to his car. He tried to unlock it, but the key slipped out of his hand and rolled under it. He dropped to his knees and reached under the vehicle, his clothes now completely soaked. He finally managed to grab it, and then jumped into in the driver's seat. He waited a few moments, and then backed out of the parking lot and drove away.

"You can go, Hanem," she said.

He nodded and left. She placed the files securely in her desk drawer, keeping only the one belonging to the Baker girl in her hand. She had given Hanem the parts that he needed to do his job. She turned to the bookshelf and pulled *Candide* out of its place. She held it out for a few seconds, and then let it slide back in on its own. The shelf moved to the right, and she stepped into the small, closet-like space behind it. The shelf moved back into place behind her, and she knelt, putting her right knee on the cold, wooden floor.

She let her fingers graze the concrete until she found a tiny, nearly invisible button in the corner. She gently pressed it, and the floor opened a hole only big enough for one person to climb down. She took three steps down the metal ladder, and then moved the wood to its original position before continuing on. She stepped onto the stone floor below her and looked around the room.

Everything was exactly as it was supposed to be. The stone walls were still perfectly adorned with tapestries that depicted creatures described in ancient literature. There was a Persian rug on the floor and a bookshelf taking up the entirety of the back wall. A round table held many tall, unlit candlesticks in the middle of the room, and a comfortable, blood red armchair took up space to its right.

Jezebel went to a tapestry depicting an attack of the legendary Kraken on a ship sailing in a violent sea. The creature's many, all-too-realistically illustrated, tentacles were crashing ruthlessly into the vessel and mutilating it piece by piece. The few men still hanging onto pieces of plywood were nothing more than faint outlines in the night, their presence rendered unknown and insignificant in the dark waters.

She pulled the tapestry to the left gently and felt for the small hole between two stones. She stuck her index finger into it and pushed to the right. The wall slid open slowly, and she stepped into an empty, dimly lit corridor. It closed as soon as she had stepped out.

She took a torch from the wall and made her way

down the hall, passing steel door after steel door. She could hear whispers behind each one and mirthless laughter behind several, but she had learned to ignore every normally disconcerting detail of this place. She had once been afraid and ashamed to roam here freely. Now, it was no less ominous than walking through a park on a bright summer's day. Nothing felt disturbing to her, and she felt no shame as she walked by.

She finally reached the door she had been looking for and entered. It was a simple office; no adornments, decorations, or books could be found inside. The floor was bare, and there were only two chairs: one behind a steel desk and another before it. She sat in her usual seat and placed the Baker girl's file in front of her. She opened it and looked over it more thoroughly than before. She was just passing time until her next visitor showed his face.

About fifteen minutes later, the door eased open, and a short, red-haired man attempting to exude confidence took the seat in front of her. His hair was standing up at odd ends, and he seemed to have been in a rush to get dressed. Hanem stood quietly behind her, waiting for a storm he had gotten used to witnessing.

"I can't say that it's exceptionally good to see you, Rook," Jezebel said, her voice cold and expression colder.

"This isn't my fault," he said.

Jezebel's eyebrows rose. "Oh, it isn't?"

"No."

Jezebel turned to Hanem. "Do you hear that? It isn't his fault."

"Do not mock me," Rook said.

"Do you know who paid me a visit, today?" Jezebel asked.

"I didn't know that Wilson is after this case."

Jezebel turned to Hanem again. "What is it exactly

that we pay him for, Hanem?"

Hanem crossed his arms. "Exactly what he clearly isn't doing."

She pulled a file out of her desk and slid it to Rook. He read the name and slapped it down.

"This job was sloppy!"

Jezebel's mocking demeanor disappeared, and her electric blue eyes flashed. Hanem gently put his hand on her shoulder, but in no way did this calm her. Her right hand closed tightly around the pen she was holding, and she gave Rook a look so callous, so dark, that what little color he had in his face drained. He swallowed and collapsed back into the chair.

"It sounds," she said softly, "as though you are saying that I am inadequately suited to do my job."

He swallowed. "That's not what I meant."

"What is it that you meant, then?"

"I couldn't control how quickly this came out!" he said. "I'm trying to be careful, but the Elias girl was kidnapped in her apartment! That's blatant abduction, not unexplainable or unclear disappearance! I'm not a wizard, Jezebel! There's only so much I can do!"

Jezebel looked at Hanem. "From her apartment?"

Hanem looked surprised. "I specifically gave orders to have her taken from outside of a night club, not private property."

"To who?"

"Amir."

"Amir is not reckless."

"None of us are."

"Then what are you telling me?"

"Something is missing from this story."

"Throw Rook out, and then bring Amir to me immediately. Don't make me wait, Hanem."

"Do you know where he is?"

"I'm not his babysitter," she snapped. "Go."

Rook stood, but before they left, Jezebel said, "Rook, you will find out every single minute detail of Wilson's actions on this case. Don't forget that someone is always watching you. Leave."

Both men walked out, and Jezebel returned to the papers in her hand. She set the Baker file to the side and opened another. Athena Elias was a twenty-eight-year-old woman who had been a medical assistant in a surgical office for eight years. It looked like she had been doing well for herself. She had only ever been charged with a misdemeanor for driving while intoxicated, which was not grounds for an abduction or assault.

However, she had been accused of stealing prescription drugs and selling them to university students. The district attorney hadn't managed to find enough evidence to hold up in court, and she safely returned to a business based on ruining the lives of impressionable youths without a problem. After weeks of research and a great deal of observation, Jezebel had confirmed that the allegations against the woman were true. She did not, however, recall ever having Elias in her office as a client. She had seen her somewhere else, but Jezebel couldn't remember where or when. Nothing in the notes explained it.

Upon turning the page, she noticed something strange: there was no report or description of an organized disappearance. Not one word was written to clarify or even mention the method, time, or place of her abduction. Jezebel's eyes widened, and her blood ran cold. She stood and left the room. She knocked into Amir on her way out, her nose connecting with his chin. She blinked the pain away and walked back into the office with him in tow. She went around her desk, but she didn't sit down. She crossed her arms and waited for him to say something.

"Is everything alright?" he asked.

"Does the look on my face suggest that everything is alright?"

"What happened?"

She tossed the file to him.

"What is this?" he asked.

"Read it, Amir."

Amir picked it up and sat on the edge of her desk. He furrowed his eyebrows and said, "We had nothing to do with it. She disappeared before I could make a move. I assumed her case was dead."

"Why is this the first I'm hearing of it? Is anyone investigating this? Why the hell didn't you tell me?"

"I thought you knew."

"Liar."

"I swear."

"Swears mean nothing."

"I left that report on Hanem's desk the night before she disappeared."

"Hanem is not careless."

"Neither am I."

"I didn't say you were."

"How did you find out about this?"

Jezebel sat down. "A detective chasing the Elias case suspects that I was behind this. He came into my office, today. He thinks I had something to do with her disappearance. I've never seen him before, but I think that he may have been tracking me for a very long time, now."

"Did he outwardly accuse you?"

"I don't think he has enough evidence to do that yet. He tried to intimidate me into letting something slip."

"The one time we're actually innocent."

"Isn't that always the way?"

"And Rook?"

"Is getting fired, but that can wait."

"This isn't my fault, Jezebel."

"You should have told me."

He dropped the file back onto the desk. "Do you believe me when I tell you that I thought you knew?"

"I'll choose to believe you."

"That isn't the same thing."

"Don't be pedantic."

"What are you thinking?"

"I have to do something about Wilson."

"Such as?"

She picked up the picture on her desk and looked at it quietly. The girl in the photograph looked so innocent. Her smile suggested that she had never done anything wrong in her life, and she was so beautiful. It was difficult to imagine her doing any of the crimes she had been accused of.

Jezebel hesitated for a moment, and then said, "It's unfortunate, what happened to these girls."

"You care?" he asked.

She ignored the question. "Do they have families?"

"Most likely. Do you want to give them money?"

"Not exactly."

She left the room.

THREE

Jezebel scrutinized the room. She had decided not to choose a venue off of her own property for the event. It was big enough that it could encompass a vast celebration hall that easily fit about one hundred and fifty people. She had decided not to make it a big affair; Charity and philanthropy greatly lacked in candor when displayed ostentatiously. Simplicity, albeit a little expensive, was seen as true sincerity. Regardless of her real motives or feelings, her intentions needed to be thought of as pure by all of those who closely watched her.

The room was beautiful, even unadorned. It was circular, denying all guests within it any successful attempt to hide in a corner, out of direct line of vision. It was technically two stories high, and open balconies lined the walls all around the room. They looked out onto the floor below, and the mahogany rails were only waist high, making them slightly dangerous. Leaning too far over would lead to a nasty fall, but many people still braved it. It was too beautiful a sight to miss.

The balconies were reached by two grand staircases

that descended toward the floor and ended on either side of a raised dais that was something like a stage. The polished wooden rails were garlanded with fresh white roses, and the steps were a black marble with faint hints of white. The floor was another optical illusion, this one less disabling than the other. It depicted black and white striped coils, wrapping in circles into themselves, getting smaller with each turn, until they created a vortex that pulled the beholder's eyes into it, sometimes unwillingly. It was captivating, and he who looked at it from above was overcome with an intense feeling of being sucked into the center. Some people were not as spellbound as others, but children were not allowed to go up alone or look down.

The ceiling was painted to resemble the night sky. Its constellations and stars were brighter than those that were regularly found in the blanket of ink that overtook the earth. They were like brilliant spirits making their mark on the world. The midnight purple backdrop accented their intense white light so greatly that they were hauntingly beautiful. Small, faint circles illustrating many moons graced the sky and were lost in the stars. Jezebel often found herself staring at it for several minutes at a time, lost in space, rife with thoughts of fantastic impossibilities that could never come true for her. They were just dreams.

Round tables were scattered around the room. They were covered in centerpieces, pictures, and other decorations. Jezebel had no part in choosing any of it. She had no interest in aesthetic design. None of it meant anything to her. Others took care of it and she barely noticed. She contributed nothing but the money.

Jezebel had previously been questioned about how she had come to have such a fortune. The salary of a psychologist couldn't possibly fund any of it, but she had always been quick to answer. She had long ago made it known that she was the heiress of a very wealthy baron in Southern Italy, who happened to be her great-grandfather. She invested her wealth in various projects after her grandfather's death, and her wealth grew. There was truth to the story, but her inheritance had been less than enough to buy a decent car, let alone a mansion.

Eleven people were seated at each table, one of which was designated for seating the families of the girls who had gone missing. Jezebel made a note to visit them before the night came to a close. Presently, she decided it was time to say a few words to the guests whose company she had no desire to be in.

She climbed the four steps onto the raised platform and stopped at the podium. The room lapsed into silence.

"I generally begin speeches by expressing how wonderful it is to see you all, but under the circumstances, I think a simple welcome will suffice."

She looked around at the faces that appeared to be listening to her intently and wondered how many of them were actually somewhere else. If she had been given the choice, she would have joined them.

"Tonight, we honor the lives of three women, three exceptional women, who fell victim to traps of sick-minded individuals without any humanity in their hearts. Athena Elias, Laura Rant, and Amy Gellar deserve much more than a petty party, and that is why, tonight, a charity fund in their name has been created to support battered women and children on the streets of New York City. It is with great pride that I take part in this effort, and I can only hope that this, in some small way, can quell the pain of their families. I pray that, wherever they are, God is keeping them safe and will soon bring them home. Thank you for coming, everyone."

Jezebel left the stage and made her way to the gold-clad table at which the young women's families sat. Two mothers, two sisters, a brother, a grandmother, and one father were there, all of them having shed some amount of tears. None of them were present for Athena. Jezebel briefly wondered how horrible a person she must have been for no one to have taken the time to be there.

She gave them a grim smile and put a hand on the shoulder of one of the mothers. "Thank you for coming, all of you."

"Thank you so much for this," the woman said.

"They deserved much more. Please, let me know if there is anything else within my power to do for you."

"Did this happen because they were bad people?" a little girl asked.

Jezebel looked at her. The girl was very short, and her brown eyes were as big as saucers. She looked terrified, as if there were monsters all around her. She was clutching a stuffed rabbit that had seen better days.

"What's your name?" Jezebel asked.

"Nina," the little girl said.

Jezebel knelt in front of her. "Sometimes bad things happen to people who don't deserve it, Nina."

"What if it happens to me?"

"Stay out of trouble, and you will be okay."

"I miss my sister, and she's gone forever."

Jezebel gave her a small smile. "The dead never truly leave us. They live on in our hearts and memories, and they only disappear when we stop loving them. Will you stop loving her?"

"Never!"

"Then she hasn't gone anywhere."

The little girl hugged her, and Jezebel pulled away seconds later. She patted the girl on the head and stood.

"No one is going to hurt a baby girl, Nina," the little girl's father said. "Isn't that right, Miss White?"

Jezebel's chest tightened. She struggled to find something appropriate to say, but she couldn't. She couldn't lie.

A small girl of about nine lay on the cold stone floor, hair disheveled and deep blue dress in shambles. Rivers of tears had fallen from her eyes, but she was too afraid to make a sound. Her pale skin clearly exposed every mark, every tear, every scar that had come to find her. Her innocent green eyes displayed pure terror, and she was curled into a ball, shaking.

She was looking at the only other person in the room: a teenaged girl whose hair and eyes mirrored her own. It was as if they were one person at two different stages of life. One of them was actively suffering childhood trauma of sorts, and the other found herself in the face of her first decision to save only herself.

A short, thin man with yellowing eyes approached her. A mocking smile spread across his face, revealing sharp, blackened teeth. Behind them rested a thick, puce slab of meat that had been created to serve as a tongue, and he used it to wipe the thick drool that had begun to seep from the right side of his mouth. He rasped heavily, chest rising and falling irregularly as he breathed from his mouth; his nose looked as though it was simply too small for any substantial intake of air.

The expression on his face was one of true pleasure and excitement. He knelt next to the child and grazed her face with decrepit hands, skin hanging loosely over bone. He held her hand for a few moments, gently rubbing the inside of her palm. He pulled her up and forced her into a warm embrace. She was paralyzed in fear, unable to move or make a sound.

He held her with one arm, and then reached his right arm into his back pocket. He retrieved a small knife and slowly brought his arm back to its original position around her. His hold was extremely gentle, as if he were a father caressing his daughter after a nightmare.

"Don't scream," he said softly.

The mother patted Jezebel's shoulder. "Thank you."

Jezebel took a deep breath and composed herself. "You have absolutely nothing to thank me for, believe me. It was very nice meeting all of you. Enjoy the rest of the event."

She went to pour herself a drink, she didn't make it to the table. She was accosted by several enthusiastic guests. She listened and responded politely to the praise they offered her, knowing that several of them clearly did not mean a word of it. After a few minutes of entertaining the growing swarm of pretentious flies, several of whom were nothing more than undercover wasps whose only purpose was to find a reason to sting her, she extracted herself and walked away.

She finally wove her way through the crowd without being cut off by any more unwanted conversationalists. Just before she could reach the bar, she spotted Amir arguing with a short woman who looked as though she was one slice of pie away from exploding. Jezebel watched them from far away, waiting for them to finish talking. Finally, the woman walked away in a huff and Amir leaned against the wall behind him, arms crossed.

Jezebel went over and stood next to him. She didn't look his way, but she asked, "Was that Martha Marcel?"

"Bugsy Marcel's obnoxious sister, yes."

Jezebel raised her eyebrows. "What brought her?"

"Athena Elias was their cousin."

"I wasn't aware that the Marcel family had any emotional attachment to anyone other than themselves."

"Neither was anyone else."

"What did she want?"

"To convince me to give her an honorable mention, as she and Elias were just so close."

"Why didn't she sit at the table with the families, then?"

"Claimed she was shy."

"Martha is never shy."

"There's no reason to believe a word out of her mouth, regardless. Did you invite her?"

"No. Is her brother here?"

"Not that I know of."

"Find me if he is."

He nodded, and she walked away. She finally made it to the bar without being stopped. She decided to drink only water, as she valued her sobriety. She took the glass and turned to find her seat and collided with someone. The water spilled out all over her and the cup fell out of her hand. Someone handed her a napkin, and she looked up to find none other than Detective Asher Wilson standing there. He was giving her an insincere apologetic look. She wasn't at all surprised to find that he had come—irritated, but not surprised.

"I'm sorry," he said. "That was unintentional."

"Okay," she said.

"So, Miss White," he said. "We meet again."

"A competent detective would have deduced that we would run into each other at my own party."

"Only being cordial."

"I'm sure."

"Very well put together."

"Thank you, but I don't recall inviting anyone from your department. This is a private event."

"I assumed that our invitation had gotten lost in the mail."

"Are you trying to have me report you, Detective? It seems like you think I won't."

"I'm not so naïve."

"Then why are you in my house?"

"This technically isn't your house."

"I doubt your superiors will see it that way."

"I'm only here to make the support of the police department known. You look lovely, by the way. That dress looks stunning on you."

"I find flattery to be the lowest form of mockery."

"It isn't flattery if it's truth."

Jezebel was distracted by the interruption of a woman she had always found unpleasant. She was very short, coming up only to about Jezebel's nose, and extremely thin. She clearly had very little upper body strength. She could never hope to adequately defend herself in a fight, but this didn't stop her from being snarky and condescending to everyone she spoke to. Her smile was never genuine, and her compliments were always laced with an insult. Her invitation had only stemmed from the political status of her husband, and Jezebel had a feeling that even he found her intensely annoying. At every event they attended together, he was far away from her for almost the entire night. At that moment, he was nowhere to be found.

Nevertheless, Jezebel smiled.

"Mickey! So wonderful of you to come," she said.

"Oh, thank you so much for the invitation," the woman said. "It's a delightful event."

"I thought it was the least that could be done in their name."

"You've managed the least very well."

"I appreciate that."

"The room is smaller than I thought it would be."

"Or maybe you need glasses."

The fake smile melted off the woman's face and she turned her nose up in the air. "I'll be on my way, then. I'm going to need a drink if I'm going to spend an entire night here."

"Enjoy the event."

She walked away, and Wilson said, "You're much less attractive when you're being kind."

She didn't turn to him. "Feigning kindness, I'm sure you mean."

"I wouldn't protest that assumption."

"You're addicted to proving that I'm some kind of storybook villain, aren't you, Wilson?"

"Am I your enemy?"

"I don't have enemies. I have nuisances."

"I'm not entirely sure that even you believe that."

"But I am entirely sure I don't care."

"Who is that man you were just talking to?"

"Who convinced you that you have any right to demand information from me?"

"Only making conversation."

"Don't."

"You have colorful friends."

"You have colorful ways of pretending not to blatantly suspect that I'm a criminal."

"One of the prettiest I've seen."

"Such a way with words."

"I've been told."

She turned her head toward him and asked, "Why is it that you suspect me so much?"

"We're talking about this openly?"

"I've always hated dancing."

He made a harsh, bark-like sound that she could only assume was meant to be a laugh. "You're not alone there."

"My question stands."

"I've seen enough evidence against you and the people who work for you to nearly confirm what I think."

"The people who work for me?"

"I have seen how quickly they take orders from you. You are not alone in this."

"Alone in what?"

"You tell me."

She looked down at her drink, grazing the top of the glass lightly with her fingertips. "'Why then should witless man so much misweene, that nothing is but that which he hath seen?'"

"The Faerie Queen."

She blinked and looked at him. "You read it?"

"You said it was your favorite book."

"I did not."

"I have good instincts."

"If that were true, you wouldn't be stalking me."

"I was trying to impress you."

"In love with me, are you?"

"I might be inclined to pay you a personal visit in prison."

"I do look stunning in orange."

"In everything, I'd say."

"You are very annoying."

"Kindest thing you've ever said to me."

"In the two instances we've seen each other. Those odds aren't so bad, Detective."

"I've seen you before."

"You're a thorough stalker."

"There's nothing wrong with taking my work seriously."

"No, there isn't. You're just too stupid to be in this line of work."

"Your insults are transparent."

"Your opinion is irrelevant."

"I'm going to miss this banter when you're behind bars."

"If you manage to catch me, that is."

"So there's something to catch."

"If you can."

Hanem suddenly appeared in front of her and muttered in her ear. "We have impatient company."

"Can it wait?" she whispered back.

"They can. You can't."

"Find someone to keep an eye on *him*." She moved away and looked at Wilson. "Would that I could stay and continue this conversation, but I have other people to talk to. Can't say it's been a pleasure."

She didn't wait for an answer before walking away.

Jezebel disappeared through the double doors and out into the garden. The hall was not attached to the house. She found it too intrusive. The building stood about three thousand feet away from the rear of her home, a garden full of rosebushes and other beds of flowers between them. A winding path led from the Hall's front doors to the thick, stone back door to the main house. It was lined with lights that turned on once the sun had fully disappeared from the sky, making it glow brightly in the night.

She went inside the main house and shut the door carefully behind her. She found herself in a small room that served as an empty study. She walked out of it and headed down the hall to the master staircase. She went up two floors and entered the only room at the top. She slammed the heavy wooden door behind her and found three men waiting for her in silence. Two of them were seated, and the third was Amir, jaw clenched, and arms crossed, leaning against a wall. She went around them all and stood behind her desk.

She looked at the African American man sitting in the left chair. "I was under the impression that we have already come to a reasonable understanding, Jules."

"And I was under the impression that this understanding has not been breached, Jezebel."

"Where is Athena Elias?"

"I assumed it was you."

"So did I, until two nights ago, when I found out that not only am I suspected for being associated with this woman's murder, but I am somehow also *innocent*."

"Why should we believe you?" the mousy-haired man with a fake tan in the other chair asked. "You're a treacherous snake."

"I don't care about your opinion."

"Perhaps you should."

"And if I don't?"

"There are consequences for even *your* actions, White."

"Maybe, but not on my property."

"You have about as much immunity as anyone, or maybe less."

"And you have about as much resemblance to your supposed namesake as festering mold, Bugsy."

Bugsy stood up. "I won't have you insult me."

"You are in my office. Only I decide what is or isn't said in here."

"You do not control me."

"In here I control everyone."

He saved their ears the stupidity of any more words by stomping childishly out of the room. Jezebel turned to Jules.

"Have you been dealing behind my back, Jules?"

"I'm surprised and upset that you're questioning my loyalty, Jezebel. I have never betrayed you."

Bugsy stormed back in and said, "I'd just like to say that you so often forget that you are a *woman* and are considerably weaker than the rest of us. You could easily be severely injured, or even murdered, because you're weaker than us all."

Amir swiftly went to him and snatched him by his wrinkled blue shirt, holding him like a rag doll. He lifted Bugsy up to his face, but before he could do anything,

Jezebel stopped him.

"Put him down," she said.

Amir violently let go of the man. He stumbled back enough times that he almost collapsed, but he grabbed the back of a chair to catch himself before he fell onto the floor. He stood up and composed himself, and Jezebel went around her desk and stood uncomfortably close to him. He was so short that they were nearly in each other's direct line of vision.

"What was that?" she asked softly.

He cleared his throat and took two steps away from her. "I am not afraid of you, White."

"That makes you stupid, not brave."

Before Bugsy could speak, someone knocked on the door roughly. Amir opened it, and Hanem walked in quickly. Amir's brother, Adel, followed him in. Adel was holding a black suitcase. Hanem closed the door and locked it. Jezebel looked away from Bugsy and waited for Hanem to speak.

"Jezebel—" Hanem began.

"What is that?" Bugsy interrupted.

"Leave my office," Jezebel said to him.

"Excuse me?"

"You heard what I said. You disrespected me once. You won't do it again. There are several methods I'm capable of using that can cause you quite a lot of pain right now, if you don't leave."

Bugsy looked at Jules. "Are you coming?"

"If I haven't overstayed my welcome, no," Jules said.

"I think you ought to stay, Jules," Hanem said. "Bugsy, if you value what is left of your health, you will get the hell out of this house completely before Adel opens that suitcase."

"Are you attempting to scare me?"

"You are already scared."

"Don't talk down to me."

"Get out," Jezebel said.

"Fine." He stalked out of the room. Hanem closed the door behind him and stuck a chair under the handle.

"Why did you send him out?" Jules asked.

"Open the suitcase, Adel," Hanem said.

Everyone looked at Adel. He placed the suitcase on the desk, and then covered his hands with black gloves before opening it. He took out the contents, set them on the desk, and moved away to show them. Before them was a silver revolver, along with one bullet and four shells.

There was an unsteady pause as every single person in the room focused on the handgun sitting in front of them. It was clearly old and abused. The grip panel was defaced so significantly that it was difficult to see the brown color it had been at some point in time. Both the crane and the muzzle were chipped, and the cylinder seemed too loose to be wholly functional. It looked familiar. No one who worked closely with her would ever hold something so battered, but still, it was like she had seen it before. She couldn't remember where.

"I've seen this before," Jezebel said.

"That doesn't surprise me," Hanem said.

"Why?"

"This is a murder weapon," Adel said.

"Athena Elias is dead," Hanem said.

"How do you know that?" Amir asked.

"Her body was found in Pasadena," Hanem said.

"California?" Jezebel asked.

"Yes."

"Was she alone?" Amir asked.

"Yes, but from what I've learned about her, that isn't unusual."

"Do you have any idea who did it?" Jezebel asked.

"Yes, but you won't like the answer."

"Let me be the judge of that."

"You want to take this, Jules?"

Everyone looked at him, but Jules seemed completely dumbstruck, staring at the weapon in total silence, as if expecting it to move or speak. His light brown eyes were wide, and his mouth was hanging open in disbelief. He recognized it, and hearing what it had done had rendered him incoherent.

"What?" he asked.

"What could possibly be confusing you?" Hanem asked.

"I don't understand this."

Amir looked at him and spoke slowly, as if he was talking to a child. "Athena Elias is dead."

"Her heart has stopped beating," Adel said.

"Someone shot her in the head and chest," Hanem said.

"She's been stuffed into the ground," Amir said.

"Not necessarily," Jezebel said.

"Cremation is very expensive," Amir said. "They wouldn't waste their money on it."

"Who are 'they?'" Adel asked. "No one in her family even showed up here, tonight."

"Maybe they just live too far," Hanem said.

"Or they don't care," Amir said.

"This isn't helping," Jules said.

Jezebel held his face roughly. "She is a lifeless female corpse formerly known as Athena Guinevere Elias."

"You know her middle name?" Jules asked.

Jezebel let go. "No. Are you with us, now?"

"I'm not an idiot."

"You were playing the part."

"Tell her about the gun, Jules," Hanem said.

"It looks familiar," Amir said.

"As head of her security, I would think that you

would immediately recognize it," Hanem said.

"Don't be a prick, Hanem," Amir said.

"This is not *possible*," Jules said.

"Are you really surprised, or are you that good at pretending to be innocent?" Hanem asked.

"Don't crucify me without evidence."

"If the shoe fits."

"That isn't my gun."

"I know, but that doesn't mean a damn thing."

"Have you run tests for fingerprinting, Hanem?" Jezebel asked.

"Yes, and I have the documentation," Hanem said and pulled a piece of paper out of the briefcase. "I don't think we need it."

"Why?" Amir asked.

"Jezebel—"

"Tell her who this belongs to, Jules," Hanem said. "Or I will."

"Bugsy. That is Bugsy's gun."

<u>FOUR</u>

Everyone in the room turned to stare at him. Jezebel's eyes narrowed. She drew closer to him and grabbed his collar, pulling him down at level with her gaze and pouring her frighteningly callous eyes into his. Though he was far taller and stronger than she was, he was not stupid enough to move. Not only were there two men in the room who would cause him severe harm at the spit of a single word from her, he was also terrified of her.

"What did you just say?" she whispered.

He couldn't summon the courage to break eye contact with her as he said, "It can't be the murder weapon. Bugsy has never spilled blood from his own gun. It would be too reckless, and he has no reason to do it."

She let go and moved away. He rubbed his neck and averted his eyes. He had only seen this expression on her face once before, and it hadn't been aimed toward him. Now, he was struggling to regulate his breathing, an embarrassing fact for an experienced gunman with a pistol lodged in his back pocket.

Jezebel was small in size, but he had met no woman who possessed an aura so akin to an angry lioness.

Hanem handed him a piece of paper. "He knew her. She was his cousin, and if I recall correctly, Bugsy is originally from Los Angeles."

"He wouldn't hide this from me," Jules said.

"Exactly why I'm questioning what *you* are hiding," Jezebel said.

"I had no part in this."

"Where were you the night she disappeared?"

"With my sister and her husband. They will vouch for me."

"You know better than I that an alibi means nothing."

"I had no part in this," he repeated. "Just let me talk to Bugsy."

"I'm afraid that won't be possible," Jezebel said. "Amir."

Amir asked no questions. He just left.

"Hanem, wait twenty-four hours and then give Rook the location of the body. Also, I want fifteen files on my desk by midnight. Right now, I have guests to cordially throw out."

"Jezebel," Hanem said.

"You know I have no choice, Hanem."

"I'm worried about you."

"Don't."

"Listen to me."

"No."

"Jezebel."

She sighed. "What?"

"Don't you worry about your soul?"

"What's left of it, you mean."

She left the room and went back out to the ballroom. She entered through the double doors and was greeted by a burst of sound. The crowd seemed louder now than it had been before. She walked toward the bar once again, only to be intercepted by a man she had only seen in shadows and behind closed doors. Instead of tapping her gently, he nearly hurled his body in front of hers, causing so hard a collision that she stumbled backward. His feet, however, remained securely planted on the ground. He was much larger than she was, and he was coated by layers of fat rather than muscle, big as a boulder and elastic as a rubber ball.

The enormous and repugnant man's features seemed much sharper—perhaps due to such bright lights—and his expression was angrier than she usually found it to be. His eyes were narrowed, and the thick coating of fat under his eyebrows forced the lids to sag further on their own, causing their brown color to be nearly lost on the naked eye.

"I did not invite you," she said.

"I can go where I please."

"I disagree. There are many places with doors you couldn't fit through."

"You aren't as witty as you think you are."

"Why are you here?"

"Not happy to see me?"

"Can't say I am, no."

"You have been difficult to reach, lately."

"And this was your final means of contact?"

"Something like that."

"Call Hanem on Monday. I'm busy."

"You will listen to me."

"Don't you dare give me orders."

"Because I'm in your sad excuse for a home?"

"Because I can hurt you, Lanyard."

"Use those scare tactics on someone else, White."

"What is it that you so desperately want to talk about?"

"You aren't keeping up—"

She interrupted him with a sigh and turned to leave, but he held her arm and continued, "—your end of the bargain. We have a deal. Fifteen per four weeks. You'll find that tonight marks the last day before your deadline, and we have all received only four."

"You know that there is something strange going—"

"Your insistence on hand-picking is keeping you from—"

"Do *not* insinuate that I'm incapable of doing my job. "

"I didn't say that, but you are allowing your emotions as a woman—"

She slapped him hard across his face. "You refer to me as weak because I am a woman, but don't seem to have noticed that the only thing proving your supposed manhood has been rendered nonexistent due to the rolls of lard that cover it. You shouldn't be so quick to judge me because of my gender when it's no longer possible to determine yours."

"You disgusting whor—"

"Be careful what you say to me. You are in my house. If you value whatever is left of your health, leave."

"There is nothing you can do to hurt me in the middle of so a large crowd."

"So afraid of me that you wouldn't catch me on my own?"

"No, but I have met your security detail. I am not stupid."

"Beg to differ."

"I could make you beg for a myriad of things."

"You would have to be capable of pleasing a woman in order to manage that."

"You're not worth it."

"Your judgment isn't sound enough for your

opinion to matter."

"Your tongue will get you in trouble, one day."

"I doubt that. I'm too good with it."

"Because you are nothing but a s—"

"Finish that sentence, and the presence of this crowd will no longer matter to me or anyone who works for me. You are a disgusting, useless pack of lard. Leave me the hell alone."

Lanyard grabbed her arms and pulled her toward him. She tried to wrench herself free, but he refused to let go. He dragged her back out of the hall and shut the door behind them. He pushed her up against the cold wall and stepped close enough to her that she could feel his breath on her cheeks. She winced and turned her face away, but he wouldn't have it. He held her face and brought his level to hers.

"Let me go," she said.

"No one's here to listen to you scream."

She tried to pull away again, but he didn't let go. "It doesn't make you any less of a criminal, you know, choosing them individually. You are just as evil, just as vicious, and just as vile as the rest of us. The only difference between us is your delusion that saving those who *you* think are worth it makes you in some way heroic. You aren't any form of deity to make that decision, especially because you're exceptionally bad at it. No one will give you a break for any of these problems, because you created them for yourself. It could have been avoided, had you accepted that nothing you can say will absolve you of what you're doing, and for profit no less."

"Get out."

He let go of her and stepped back. "With pleasure."

He turned and waddled away. She took a deep breath and looked around to see if anyone had witnessed the altercation. No one was outside. She fixed her clothes and dusted herself off. She ran a hand through her hair, and then walked back into the hall again.

She leaned against a wall quietly and watched everyone else as they interacted with each other without a care in the world. She averted her gaze to the masterpiece that was her ceiling.

She wasn't afraid. There was nothing for her to be afraid of. She had committed herself to this belief already, but even then, the screaming rang in her ears repeatedly. She remembered the girls being dragged into the shadows. She remembered watching the brutality and unnatural malice from her dark corner across the room. She remembered the disgusting smell of the pots they chose to use instead of toilets. She remembered being forced to stand between them, inhaling the revolting scent of human waste while being tortured with the sounds of pain from down the hall.

How could she possibly forget? She stood there again, reliving every moment repeatedly, each time with more anguish than the last. She remained frozen in her corner, and suddenly, the echoes of screams were no longer distant. She found herself watching with apparent indifference as more women were wrapped in chains and dragged across the floor in front of her.

She didn't care, as long as they didn't touch her.

He came and stood next to her. She knew who it was, and she knew what he wanted to say. He wanted to tell her that it was her fault. As soon as she chose to make a deal with the devil, she had damned the other girls to hell on earth. No matter how much regret filled her, no matter how hard she tried to fix it, there could be no forgiveness for what she had been a part of.

She gritted her teeth and ignored him. He did not open his mouth, but a flutter of an eyelid later, the creature slashed him from navel to nose without stepping out of the dark. He choked, and blood spurted from the wound. Warm, red liquid spilled from his mouth, and his eyes rolled back. He crumpled to the floor.

She didn't care to look at the scene for longer than a second. It didn't disturb her. She had grown accustomed to the bloodshed. She didn't have to see the thing to know exactly where it was, and she was no longer afraid of it. It was far less ominous to her than it once was. Time had taken its toll.

The disgusting sound of its tongue lapping up the blood gushing from his body was familiar, now. It was almost normal. From the corner of her eye, she saw it peel his skin slowly and toss it in a pile by her feet. She heard his bones crack and shatter as the thing tore them cleanly out of his limbs to suck the marrow dry. It never enjoyed the flesh itself. The bones and blood were what brought the frightening and mirthless grin to the thing it unjustly called its face.

It crawled up her left arm and nested on her shoulder, breathing hot air into her ear. Its talons dug into her shoulder, drawing enough blood to slip down her left arm. It bit the back of her earring and spit it out of its mouth so violently that it hit the opposite wall and fell into darkness. She still wasn't perturbed. She had learned that reacting in any way always led to nasty and painful consequences. No matter how long they were together, it would show her no mercy.

It nudged her shoulder, and she finally emerged from her corner toward a room at the end of the hall. It was once extremely difficult to navigate the darkness, but she no longer needed light. She did not know what her surroundings looked like in reality. All that she knew were the illusions she had dreamt up on her own. She had no idea what was on the walls, the floor, or the ceiling. It was always night, here. The sun was not permitted to shine, and she doubted that there were any windows for it to shine through, regardless.

She entered the small room and sat on the bed. Before the creature could make a single move, she heard someone shout something in a language she still could not recognize. It hopped off of her shoulder and left, leaving her alone for the night for the first time in what seemed like ages.

In an instant of uncharacteristic recklessness, she stood and went to the door. She pulled it open only enough to let her body fit through, and then slipped down the hall. She had never been further than the room she slept in before. She wasn't permitted to go very far unaccompanied. The silence was replaced by the sound of her own beating heart. It was louder than any noise that had ever graced her ears.

She ran her fingers along the wall to her left gently as she moved forward and felt an irregularity in the surface. She moved closer and rubbed it, realizing that it was now wood instead of stone. She felt around for a handle, and when she found it, she turned her entire body to face it.

She knew what could be behind it but for once, her curiosity overcame her fear. She turned the handle carefully, cracked the door open barely an inch, and listened. The voices were arguing, but she couldn't understand what was going on. She heard her name, followed by several blood-curdling screams, and then shut the door immediately. She made it back down the hall again and felt around for her own door's handle. She found it and knocked into another door. When she touched the handle, she realized that this wasn't her room.

She gathered her courage once again and opened it a few more inches than she had the first one. All she could hear were screams and mirthless laughs. She pushed it a sliver more and spotted a woman who had fallen onto her back. A nail was stuck in her chest, and she was breathing in short, strained gasps. The nail was rusted and dirty, and the blood oozing from the wound was thick and heavy. The woman gave her a pleading look, but she would have to physically enter the room to help her. The courage began to fall away, and the need for self-preservation took over. She shut the door and quickly walked away, leaving the woman there to die.

A hand rested on her arm, and she jumped. She blinked a few times and looked down from the ceiling. Asher Wilson was standing in front of her, eyebrows raised and holding a drink in his left hand. He was attempting to seem concerned, but she could tell it wasn't genuine.

"Are you alright?" he asked.

Jezebel bristled. "Don't touch me."

He moved away. "Lost in space, were you?"

"I told you to leave."

"No, you didn't. You only mentioned that you're unhappy with my presence. That isn't an order for me to go away."

She gritted her teeth. "This is borderline harassment."

"I think I've been more than cordial tonight. Nothing I have said could hardly be considered harassment."

"I want you off my property immediately."

He put his glass on a tray a server was holding and wiped his mouth with his sleeve. "I only came over to say goodbye before I left. I think I've made enough of an impact."

"In more ways than one."

"Who was that man, by the way? Interesting fellow."

Jezebel stepped closer to him and whispered, "This is my last warning, Wilson. Leave me alone, or I will not be responsible for how I react to this intrusion. You are on my property uninvited, and I won't be held accountable for anything I do to you here; if you truly suspect that I'm a criminal, you should be smarter than to think I wouldn't hurt you."

"Don't be so sensitive."

"Drop dead."

He laughed lightly and turned to leave but paused and looked back at her. "I didn't take you as one who believed in God, Miss White."

Jezebel looked him over, for the first time actually taking in his appearance. It didn't seem as though this man had made a real effort to look even reasonably adequate to attend such a formal occasion. He wore a black suit, accented with a red tie and white shirt. The first two buttons were undone, and his tie was loosened. It was improper to lazily undo his clothing in such company. Yet somehow, it looked as if that was the way the suit and tie were meant to be worn, perhaps because he was admittedly very good-looking.

She slowly diverted her gaze to the ever-present cocky grin plastered on his unshaven face, and then offered him a condescending smile.

"Even Satan believes in God, Detective."

<u>FIVE</u>

When even the most obstinate guest had gone, Jezebel once again trekked up the stairs to her office, finding comfort in the silence. She sat behind her large, mahogany desk and opened the first of the stack of files Hanem had left for her. The photo that lay above the papers tore at her frayed heart strings. This girl was so young, so beautiful, and so innocent.

Jezebel almost put the file away but cleared her throat and reminded herself that she could not allow her emotions to guide her work. Wolves often hid in sheep's clothing. A sweet photo meant nothing. She moved the picture to the side and after giving the first page a simple cursory look, was glad that she had not let the girl go. She was a monster.

Name: Mary-Jane Graham
Age: 24
Sex: Female
Occupation: Unemployed
Height: 5'3"

Eye:Brown
Race:Caucasian

Note Type: Arrest
Note: Domestic Violence; withholding access to medical care
Charges: No charge

Note Type: Arrest
Note: Domestic Violence; infliction of physical injury on partner
Charges: No charge

Note Type: Arrest
Note: Domestic Violence; child abuse
Charges: Loss of custody without visitation rights

Jezebel marked it and set it to the side. She continued looking through each file until she had twelve who fit her criteria. She wrote notes suggesting an efficient and safe course of action for each, and then set them in a small suitcase. She left the office and descended three flights of stairs. She turned left at the bottom of the staircase and passed three empty and generally useless rooms until she found herself in one of the smaller sitting rooms in the house.

She went around a forest green couch and stopped in front of the coffee table in the middle of the room. She pushed the table forward and rolled the carpet up a few inches. A small latch was embedded into the floor. She pulled it up and to her left, revealing a dark, circular hole in the floor. She took a few steps down the steel ladder and closed the trap door over her head.

She lowered herself slowly and found herself in a cloud of smoke as she dropped lightly onto the rug. The room's floor was covered with a hand-woven Persian rug, and armchairs covered with plush pillows were scattered about. The ceiling was covered in golden calligraphy of Arabic words, which she did not know the meaning of. She had never asked. She found that the true beauty of art was in its mystery. Three of the walls were lined with bookshelves, but the last was breathtakingly painted; a large, Arabian palace stood luminously in a dark, cloudless sky. There were arcs in its architecture and pillars topped with golden domes. Stained glass windows fit into each pillar, and a golden staircase led to its front door.

Amir, his brother, and three other men were inside. A thick smoke emanated from the hookahs each man had partnered with. The room was dimly lit, and soft music played in the background. A few of them were falling asleep, the hoses left lifelessly in their hands or loosely in their mouths. Amir lay comfortably across the floor, just reading. She stood and watched him for a few moments.

He looked up. "Jezebel."

"Amir."

"I expected you earlier."

She offered him a small smile and leaned on the back of a chair. "After spending so many years together, I would think that you knew by now that I never meet anyone's expectations."

"Not on purpose."

"No, not on purpose."

"Is that for me?" he asked and pointed to the suitcase in her hand.

She avoided the question and picked up the book he was reading.

"What is this?" she asked.

He took it back and showed her the cover. "You know that I'm not as godless as you are."

"I am not godless."

"I try harder."

"You are a killer. What are you hoping to get out of reading this? Some kind of forgiveness?"

"No," he said, his dark eyes bearing more humanity than she was accustomed to seeing in him.

"What are you looking for, then?"

"Peace."

"Did you find it?"

"Sometimes."

"How uncharacteristically pious of you."

"Piety has different definitions."

"If you say so."

"Again, is that for me?"

"For Hanem."

"And the Koreans."

"I knew you disliked Hanem."

"I don't dislike Hanem. It just bothers me that you trust him more than you trust me."

"I do not."

"You would rather give him free reign on making plans, even though I have worked for you much longer than all of them."

"You all have your uses."

"Violence versus intellect."

"You're being unfair."

"You don't trust me."

"I do trust you."

"That isn't how it seems."

Jezebel set the briefcase down. "Are you questioning me?"

"I know better."

"Then make your point."

"The Brazilians have their beauty. The Koreans have their intelligence. My kind, you use for—"

"Hanem is talented in developing ideas, not

executing them. You're much better suited for carrying out complicated tasks and, yes, physical confrontation. You chose that path for yourself when you decided to build your strength as much as you have. I didn't force that on you."

"And anyone with the tiniest bit of color takes the blame every time you are nearly caught."

"Are you afraid of using labels, Amir? I never took you for someone who cares about being politically correct."

"Jezebel."

She sighed. "Our justice system is a game, and I have to play it with every trick I have up my sleeve, regardless of how racist it may seem. Every single one of you knew what you are here for before you started. Don't forget that they are very highly-paid for it and getting them out is an option I always give them, if they choose to risk becoming escaped felons."

"And *you* can get away with murder."

"As long as I have someone else to frame, I probably can."

"You lump us together based on ethnicity."

"I have never generalized by race. I gave you and Hanem free reign to choose who to hire for your respective teams, and neither of you chose a soul outside of your own ethnicity. I didn't make either of you do anything. You are birds of a feather, and you flocked together all on your own."

"I have known you a very long time."

"My condolences."

He didn't laugh. "I'm worried about you."

The amusement drained from her face. "I don't need anyone to worry about me as if I'm a weak little—"

"Are you starting to enjoy this?"

The question caught her off guard. "Of course not."

"It isn't affecting you the same way it once did."

"Desensitization is real."

"And dangerous."

"Well, flirting with danger is my favorite thing to do."

"I know, and I'm here to keep you out of danger."

"Stay out of my life."

"You hired me to protect you."

"I hired you as head of security, not a babysitter."

"You hired me as head of security, not an audience."

"'Audience' is plural."

"Don't change the subject."

"This conversation will take us nowhere."

"Because you listen to no one but yourself."

She turned to the wall and touched the painted golden gate. She pushed it, and the wall swung forward, giving the illusion that she was actually entering the palace. She turned back to Amir.

"Reckless enough to keep the door open?"

She didn't wait for an answer. She walked through and let the palace door return to its place behind her. She pulled her sweater tighter at the sudden drop in temperature and began to make her way down the hall.

Her footsteps echoed loudly, filling the corridor with a sound fit for a horror film. It was not so late that everyone would have vacated the area, and new people had been freshly taken and brought here for storage She stopped in front of a steel door and pushed her key into the lock. She opened the door and stepped into the blindingly luminescent room.

In a wooden chair chained to the stone wall, was Bugsy Marcel. He was dressed in a gray suit, complete with a crumpled white shirt and loosened, tousled blue tie. He hadn't come without a fight. He looked exhausted. There were the dark circles under his eyes, and all color seemed to have been sucked out of his face. Though the temperature of the room was neither cold nor hot, he looked frozen.

Bugsy looked up at her, and his eyes lit up in anger. "LET ME GO, YOU BITCH!"

A small, patronizing laugh escaped her, and she sat in the only other chair in the room, barely a few feet away from the man. He flinched and backed away, but she inched forward with the chair. There wasn't much room to put any helpful distance between them.

"Did you really think that I wouldn't find out?" she asked.

"I have no idea what you're on about."

"I think you do."

"Your thoughts don't matter."

"Even in a position of weakness, you can't keep your mouth from getting you into trouble.

"I am never weak, you disgusting—"

Jezebel shot out of her chair so quickly that the rest of his sentence died in the back of his throat. She slapped him across his face with the back of her left hand so hard that her ring imprinted on his skin.

"Do not insult me again."

"I am not afraid of you."

Jezebel's face melted into a small, innocently eerie smile as she said, "I don't mean to give you a reason to be, Bugsy."

"Stop playing with me."

She drew closer to him. She gently swept up the few hairs that fell loosely over his face, touching his cheek lightly in the process. All color had drained from his face, and his skin was ice cold. He almost trembled under her touch, but he didn't open his mouth to say a word against it.

She laughed and leaned down to whisper in his ear, "The devil himself wouldn't toy with me, Bugsy."

It was as if he had lost his voice. The gentleness in her voice was disconcerting. She looked back into his eyes and furrowed her eyebrows. Her smile crashed into a cold frown, a transition so fast that his heart jumped, and tremors travelled up and down his spine. His blood ran cold. Suddenly, everything blurred but the sharp picture that was the woman sitting in front of him.

"Tell me why you killed her," she said.

He couldn't speak.

"Tell me why you killed her, Bugsy."

He didn't make a sound.

She took a few steps back and kicked the chair out from under him. He fell over, his narrow eyes as wide as physically possible. His face hit the stone floor roughly, and blood trickled from his nose. His chest rose and fell rapidly as he struggled to regulate his breathing.

"Tell me why you killed her."

"She-She tried to kill me first," he stuttered.

In one fluid motion, her right foot jammed itself into the pit of his stomach, and he coughed up blood.

"Funny how that doesn't sound very true to me."

He didn't say a word.

She knelt in front of him and held his face gently. "Go on, tell me the truth. Take deep breaths, so you don't faint. I want you to make it through this. Don't you trust me, Bugsy?"

"She's been giving my sister drugs!"

She let go and sat cross-legged in front of him. "The one who came into my house uninvited just a few hours ago?"

"Yes! She is the only sister I have, Jezebel!"

"I thought you and your sister were estranged."

"We are only private about our relationship."

"And what is the nature of that relationship?"

Anger tore through his fear, and he yelled, "Don't make accusations when you don't know what the hell you're talking about!"

"Even you could do better than that creature."

"DO NOT TALK ABOUT MY SISTER!"

Jezebel stood and looked down at him. "Someone will escort you out of here in the morning. Do not give me a reason to bring you back, Marcel."

She made to leave, but he said, "You are nothing but a selfish, deluded, cheap whor—"

Jezebel's foot made forceful contact with his stomach, again. More blood erupted from his throat, and he gasped for breath. The blood turned into vomit, and thick liquid splashed onto the floor. She took a few steps away quickly to keep it from touching her shoes.

"Do not give me a reason to bring you back, Marcel," she repeated. "I don't have the patience for the same meeting twice."

He couldn't quell his coughing enough to manage a response, and she left the room, letting the door slam behind her.

Jezebel made her way back down the hall and turned right, looking to find solitude in her office. Thoughts rushed through her mind as she walked, and she struggled to keep up with each before it melted into another. She was too busy trying to push through her anger to pay attention to where she was going.

She stopped at a door and absently pushed it open. It took a moment for her to realize that in her inattentive state, she had walked into a room that she had been avoiding for many long years. Up until that moment, she had been successful.

Her heart plummeted to the soles of her feet at the scene in front of her. Three women, including Linda Baker, were passed out on cots on the floor. They were fully clothed and clean, but their hands and feet were chained. Even in their slumber, their faces held such deep hopelessness and fear that she was nearly driven to wake them and take them home. It had been so long. She had gotten used to the work she was doing because she didn't see it.

The room she stood in was far colder than any place she had ever visited. Her fingers and toes felt so frozen that they were in danger of falling off entirely. The shirt she wore was so thin she would not feel any colder if she decided to take it off, which was a display she knew would be welcomed by all of the degenerate brutes behind her. Her cold-hearted company caused the temperature in the room to be even colder than it was on its own.

One of the men shoved her forward violently, and she had become so weak from malnourishment and abuse that she stumbled forward, almost dropping the gun. She heard a hiss behind her but chose not to turn. She didn't trust her face to remain apathetic if she laid her eyes on the creature unprepared. Revulsion was difficult to hide well.

The girl at her feet was a disheveled, chaotic compilation of bones and unkempt hair. Her skin was covered with grime that gave her naturally dark complexion an unattractive tint of murkiness. Several small cuts covered her sunken cheeks, and her chin was caked with dried blood. The hole in the girl's nose that once held a lovely ring was inflamed and infected, a puce bubble of pus growing at the edge of the opening. The girl's eyes were closed, hiding their color. It was so insignificant a detail, but it hung in the back of her mind stubbornly. The small things tended to matter at inappropriate times, without reason.

She raised a fresh black pistol in the air, aiming it at the unconscious girl on the floor. She worked to keep her hands from shaking and slowly placed her finger on the trigger. Her heart burrowed a pit into her stomach and throbbed painfully. Someone behind her moved her arms to ensure the bullet would connect with the soon-to-be corpse's skull.

She took a deep breath and closed her eyes. She thought the sight of the girl would be too painful to see.

Yet still, after she pulled the trigger and the fatal shot was fired, she opened her eyes to witness the bloodshed.

She felt nothing at all.

She swiftly left the room and closed the door. She leaned against the stone wall and slid to the ground, bile forming in the back of her throat. She closed her eyes. The screams continued to echo through her mind. The memory of gushing blood splattering walls around her suffocated her with guilt.

Not thirty seconds later a figure sat on the floor next to her. She didn't have to turn or open her eyes to know who it was. She was connected to him in ways no one around her could ever understand. He was the exact thing that would be her downfall if she let him in.

"Stop following me, Amir," she said.

"I didn't follow you," he said. "I was going to see Neul."

She opened her eyes and looked at him. "You're going to visit the Koreans willingly?"

"If I have to work with them, I will."

"Took you seven years to do it. Why now?"

"Because suspicious things are starting to happen, and if I'm going to protect you—"

"I do not need your protection."

He ignored her interruption and continued. "I have to know everything about everyone that has anything to do with you. That includes the Koreans and the Brazilians, no matter how I feel."

"Why do you hate them all so much?"

"Genius in the wrong hands is dangerous."

"And the Brazilians?"

"Beauty can be just as deadly as wit."

"Is that why you've dated your way through half of them?"

"I haven't dated anyone."

"Liar."

"Jealous?"

"Give me a reason to be."

"I fulfill my needs. There is only one woman I've ever wanted, and she tends to ignore me."

"Then move on."

"Would that I could."

"And yet you fancy yourself such a religious man."

"I never said that. A sinner is not a disbeliever."

"I thought you already knew everything that went on here. Is this too much responsibility for you?"

Annoyance flitted across his features. "I can handle it just fine. Things are changing, and with those changes come things that can go undetected if I'm not on top of things."

"If you can't handle it on—"

"Stop it."

"No need to be so sensitive."

"Why are you trying to annoy me?"

"Revenge."

He hesitated, and then put his arm around her. "You don't want me protecting you but I am going to do it anyway."

"If I catch you, I will hurt you."

"Promise?"

She laughed and pulled away, and then the reality of what she had just seen came crashing down onto her shoulders once more. It was all her fault, and the more she told herself that she was some kind of savior of the innocent, the more she knew that she was delusional to believe it. Every word Lanyard had said about her was true, and there was no escaping it.

"Amir."

"Jezebel."

"You've been with me since before I had all of this."

He sighed. "Why are you so intent on reminding me of the things I've done to you?"

"It's forgotten."

"You haven't forgiven me, Jezebel."

"You haven't forgiven yourself. Don't put that on me."

"What's your question, then?"

"Don't lie to me."

"I never do."

"All of you spoke a language that I can't place. Was it Persian?"

"No. It was Croatian."

"You speak Croatian?"

"Yes. What's your real question?"

She leaned her head back and looked at the ceiling. "Do you think that all of this is my fault?"

"You didn't create this system."

"I'm feeding it."

"Saving yourself is not selfish."

"I'm not the hero in this story."

"That doesn't make you a villain. It isn't one or the other. We are not in a movie. Roles are not defined as black and white in the real world."

"Then what am I?"

"Human."

She scoffed. "That's debatable."

"You just want to torture yourself."

She paused. "You never told me why you helped me get out."

"You have never been willing to hear it."

"I had you at hello?"

"If you want me to tell you why I fell for you, say so."

She got up and shook her head. "Don't."

"I wasn't going to. You asked."

"I have to go finish what I started. Don't wait up for me."

She turned to leave, but he caught her hand. He stood up and held her face in his hands. For the first time, she didn't immediately pull away.

"Don't walk away from me."

"Let go, Amir."

"What are you afraid of?"

She pushed him off. "I am never afraid."

He shook his head. "If that's what you want to believe, who am I to stop you, Belle?"

He walked away from her, and she watched him go.

After he had disappeared into the darkness she passed two more doors and stopped to knock on the third. Hanem opened it immediately. He looked exhausted but he let her in and sat behind his desk. Once upon a time he had insisted that she take his seat, but he had given up.

"Is that for me?" he asked.

She didn't hear the question; something else attracted her gaze. There was a cross hanging behind him on the wall. It was made of simple dark wood and was about the size of a medium-sized picture frame. It confused her, and in some small, strange way, it upset her.

Hanem followed her gaze and asked, "What are you looking at?"

She blinked and looked at him. "Religious?"

"How can I be, when I am in this business?"

"Then what is that?"

"Everyone believes in something, Jezebel."

"I thought that the majority of Koreans are Buddhists."

"I am Catholic, and that particular generalization is offensive," he snapped.

For once, the sharp tone didn't faze her.

"I'm sorry. I didn't mean to offend you, Hanem."

"It's fine. Is that for me?" he asked and pointed to the briefcase.

"Yes," she said and handed it to him. He opened it and removed the files. She waited as he looked over them. After a few minutes, he wrote a few notes to himself and put them in his desk.

"I'll have Amir do it himself," Hanem said.

"No," she said. "Have Adel do it."

"Why?"

"Don't question me."

"Alright."

She played with the edge of her shirt and said, "We're too close to being exposed."

"I wouldn't say that. We are all careful."

"Someone isn't."

"What do you mean?"

She let the shirt go and leaned forward, folding her hands on his desk. Her gaze poured into his eyes. A mess of many different emotions flew through her loud, dead eyes. Jezebel was the only person he had ever known that had features that both contradicted each other and somehow fit so well together.

Nothing special could be said about their color, as blue was hardly an anomaly for a woman of her race, but their intensity was unique. Her fury could light the blue orbs with an electricity that could stop the best and the worst of people in their tracks. No one was immune.

"You aren't going to like what I am about to tell you," she said.

Hanem raised his thin eyebrows. "That has never

mattered to you."

"Someone is not who they claim to be."

"If you feel that way, I can—"

"Every single person in who works with us needs to be assessed and tested, again. Every move they've made in the past three years, every file their name is mentioned in, every person they've spoken to, and every step they've taken here. I know that it will be a lot of work, but you are the only one who can do this, Hanem."

"And me? You won't check me?"

"You think that I am so naïve that I did not review you before I gave you this assignment?"

"You don't trust me!"

"No one is exempt."

"Jezebel—"

"This is not up for discussion."

Hanem shook his head. "Fine."

"I'm leaving tomorrow morning. I have some places I need to visit. I will be gone for a couple of weeks. During my time away, my office will be operating as the court requests and nothing else."

"You have contracts you can't breach."

"There are other ways to spot criminals, Hanem."

"Alright."

"I'll be back soon."

"And no one will be with you?"

"No."

"But—"

"I can take care of myself."

"You have many enemies!"

"I can handle them on my own."

"If someone assaults you, you will not have a chance. Don't be reckless because you're proud."

"I'll take my chances."

"This isn't about your gender. You are a small

person, Jezebel!"

"I'll be fine."

"Just take Amir!"

"No. I am not at Amir's mercy and I'm not desperate for him to constantly babysit me. He is not special."

"You're being unfair."

"I don't care."

"Where are you going?"

"Stop asking questions, Hanem. I'll contact you when I need to."

"And who will run the practice?"

"There are several people who are qualified to do it. It doesn't matter to me. They're all good at what they do. If someone asks you, tell them that I'm on vacation in the Caribbean."

"Okay."

She sat back in her chair. "How's your mother, Hanem?"

"She's fine."

"Isn't she sick?"

"My sister says she's alright."

"You should go see her."

"Another time. Too much is going on right now."

She stood. "There will always be too much going on, here. See your mother while you still can."

"I will."

"Goodnight."

She went to the door, but before she could leave, he asked, "Why did the cross upset you, Jezebel?"

She turned back and leaned on the cold doorframe. She returned her gaze to the cross on his wall.

"I don't know, but it's nice that you have something to believe in."

"Come back safe."

"I'll try."

<u>SIX</u>

Jezebel adjusted the sunglasses she was wearing and pulled the hood of her sweater up to cover her head. She got into the yellow taxi that had pulled up in front of her. She didn't pause to see the figure who would in a small away, be in control of her life for the forty New York minutes it would take to drive to the private plane port she had bought many years before. Until that day it had not proved to be useful.

The driver recklessly wove in and out of lanes, cutting off angry drivers and scoring many insults as he moved. The first traffic light that threatened his fast pace had no luck in stopping him. The yellow signal only seemed to push him to drive even faster, and he zipped under it mere seconds before it turned red. The officer sitting lazily in the police car near the intersection was too busy eating to make a move to pull the cab over.

The irresponsible driving didn't bother her. If he was stopped by a police officer she would simply get out of the car and move on to find another. The jeopardy his license was in did not concern her. She only cared about getting to her destination before Amir found out that she was gone, and this was a window of no more than one hour. He knew everything that went on with her, underground and above.

She had never minded before, but it was different this time. This time, she was aiming to get as far away from him as possible before he realized that she had set out to do something that endangered her safety in more ways than one.

The driver finally pulled onto the dirt road that led to the port. He drove down the dirty and unkempt path with less speed than he had before. The way his eyes shifted from side to side showed that he was nervous about where she was taking him.

Despite the fact that it was just after nine in the morning, everything around them was dark. Trees lined the road on both sides. The intense volume of the busy streets that they had just been on died almost immediately after he drove onto the path. There was an overwhelming silence in the air, and the fact that she hadn't said a word to him only intensified his discomfort.

The road finally began to give way to an open field, and she heard him exhale as soon as he saw the upcoming sunlight. Five planes were scattered across the field, and he came to a stop in front of the only one with its engine already running. No one else was there.

The driver turned and looked at her. "That's a big one for just one person, ma'am."

She didn't answer. She just stepped out of the car and close the door behind her, leaving the man to stare after her in confusion and awe. She walked to the plane's door and climbed the steps. The man standing inside the compartment closed it behind her and smiled.

"Can I bring you anything?" he asked.

"Yes. Silence."

He took the order and sat down. She took a seat by

the window and a few minutes later the pilot took off. She watched the ground disappear from under her, and then leaned her head back to stare at the ceiling. There wasn't a chance in hell that she would sleep and leave her body unguarded on such an empty plane. She needed to be alert. The lack of a crowd was dangerous. Bad things usually happened when there were no witnesses. She had many targets on her back.

Hours passed, and the plane finally began to descend. She saw the city begin to come into focus as they drew closer to Chicago's beautiful bright lights. Everything seemed to sparkle.

She got off the plane and walked into O'Hare International Airport from a door separate from the general crowd. She was led to a desk where an old, slow-working clerk stood.

"Passport," he said, his face sleepy and his voice monotonous.

She gave him her passport and waited. He lazily scanned it, his movements so slow that it felt as though time had actually slowed down to match his pace. He looked through the pages, turning each with a sluggishness that made her want to reach over the counter and wring his scrawny, pale neck.

"Cassandra Rose?" he asked.

"Yes," she said.

He handed the passport back to her and said, "Enjoy your flight."

She took it and walked away. She boarded the airplane with the other people, whose names and faces didn't register with her at all and took her seat in first class. This time she threw caution to the winds and closed her eyes. She was going to Cairo, a roughly eleven-hour flight, and arriving there unfocused or sleepy was dangerous. Two red pills down her throat later she fell asleep.

When the plane landed, she descended the stairs and went into the airport on a bus that had been waiting for them all. She made it through security and handed over her passport several more times.

When she finally made it through the airport doors, she waited to find a taxi with a driver who drove less politely than others. The fun she found in visiting Cairo was the way its residents moved through traffic. She enjoyed riding with drivers who had no problem being as vulgar as possible—the kind of vulgar where the language was colorful enough to be insulting in any tongue. She hailed a black and white cab driven by a dark-skinned man who looked intensely irritated. He stopped and opened the door for her, giving her an insincere smile.

She got in and said, "Heliopolis."

"Not a bag?" he asked, his English as broken as his door handle.

"No."

He turned back around and drove off. She didn't look out of her window. She was already familiar with this city. Instead, she examined him. He was very old, with a hairline that had been receding for years, the remaining hair the color of a dirty white crayon. He gripped the wheel with both hands, and his chair was in a position so upright that his stomach was folding into his lap. He was wearing red glasses that matched the bloodshot eyes they framed. For a moment, she actually pitied him. His life must have been so difficult.

The car stopped in the middle of a tight street in front of an eight-story building. The open door that led into it was covered in dust and grime. A tiled walkway led from the street's sidewalk and into the building, stopping at three cemented steps that led to a platform. The elevator inside could take no more than three or four people, and there was no overhead lighting of any kind.

Jezebel paid the driver and got out of the car. He drove away quickly, and she walked in. She had been in this building multiple times before. Usually, the man who guarded it was awake and met visitors at the door at all hours of the night. Today, he was nowhere to be found. She was lucky that the door was still open; it was usually closed after ten, mainly to cater to the residents' fear and paranoia in light of recent political events.

She opened the door to the elevator and stepped in. Instead of pressing a number she pulled the metal plate that held the buttons to the left. Behind it was a small security pad numbered one through ten. She punched in seven numbers and the elevator went down. A few seconds passed and then it stopped. She slid the door open, revealing another metal door. She knocked on it in three sets of four times, and it opened.

Two large, beefy men blocked her path. They crossed their arms and said something she didn't understand. One of them pushed her back into the elevator, her head slamming harshly against the metal behind her. A sharp pain shot through her, but she didn't react.

She shook off the pain and said, "Asim Marwan."

He said something in Arabic, and then grabbed her arm as if to push her back into the elevator. She jerked her arm away from him and grabbed his shirt. Her eyes displayed a wicked hostility that didn't need to be translated to be understood.

"Asim Marwan," she said again.

He hesitated, and then turned and barked something into the room behind him. A voice she knew quite well shouted something back, and the two men stepped aside. She pushed past them and surveyed the area.

The space she had entered was nothing special. It was not a beautiful hidden room, or a club of any kind, or a place where illegal games or sports were played. It was just a dimly lit, on the lower spectrum of average-sized, room with cement flooring and people in chairs scattered around. The floor was made of plain concrete and there were cracks all over it.

There were few people in the room. Women were sitting around with a few men, whispering to them and pulling on their ties flirtatiously. All of them were strangely dressed in modest clothing. The only thing that drew her attention was a round table in the middle of the room surrounded by three men. Papers were scattered over it, and they were talking in whispers.

Jezebel walked over to them and took the last empty seat. They all looked at her, only two of them genuinely surprised. The third removed his bowler hat and set it on the table.

"You know, I could have brought you here from the airport myself if you had just told me you were coming, Cassie," he said.

"You know I don't show my hand."

"Even to your friends?"

"Don't you have to be able to trust someone, in order to be their friend?"

"I trust you, Cassie."

She laughed. "That was funny. I liked that."

"Thank you. What brings you?"

"It's too dangerous for me to work in the States right now."

"Yours is a big country. Why did you have to travel so far away when you work on the West Coast and Middle America as well?"

"I don't take chances."

"So you chose Egypt?"

"Am I not welcome?"

"You are, but you have stronger ties in London."

"It isn't easy for an American police department to

track someone in the Middle East. I can't say the same for England."

"I'm not sure if that's a compliment."

"It isn't."

"You insult my country and then ask for my help?"

"It wasn't intended as an insult, Asim."

"I want to help you, but things are more difficult here now. People make a bigger effort to stay safe because of the political unrest."

"Not as difficult as where I come from."

"No, but I still don't see that it would be very helpful for me to give you as many as you want."

"I haven't told you how many I want, yet."

"You did not come here for two or three."

"Fifteen is not too many."

"How much are you willing to pay?"

"Don't play games. How much do you want, Marwan?"

"No need to be hostile."

"Don't patronize me."

The joking demeanor faded, and he sat back in his chair. "That will be two a head."

"Pounds?"

"Dollars."

"You're joking."

"I am not."

"You're asking me for thirty thousand dollars."

"Yes."

"That's half a million pounds."

"Look how good you are at math."

"That number is ridiculous."

"You aren't bargaining me out of it."

"You're increasing the price because you know I need it."

"Say what you want."

"I can't pay that amount for just fifteen. I would be

losing money."

"Then I suppose you'll have to find someone else to help you."

"We were friends just a moment ago."

"But business is business."

She sat back in her chair and thought about it. She didn't have time to go anywhere else, and he was the best in the area. He was reliable and usually followed directions well, but he was exploiting her needs.

"Cassandra?"

"This is your final offer?"

"Yes."

"Fine."

"You're taking this surprisingly well."

"I would have done the same."

He motioned to someone to bring him a pen, and then looked back at her. "I thought that you make a point to choose carefully, Cassie. That's what you're known for."

"I expect you to do that for me."

"Excuse me?"

"You know that I never take an innocent life."

"I don't know enough about any of them to make a sound judgment on that for you."

"Figure it out."

"That is a lot of work."

"That is a lot of money you're dragging out of me."

One of the other two men asked something in Arabic, and Jezebel leaned forward onto the table and waited quietly. The conversation turned into a heated argument, and then the man stood and walked away. Asim didn't make a move to follow or call after him.

"Not happy that I'm here, is he?" she asked.

"I don't care about his opinion."

"I came here personally out of respect for our agreement."

"And that is appreciated."

Jezebel looked back at the other women in the room. They weren't at all perturbed by her gaze. It was as if she wasn't even there. It was like watching creatures that were simply modeled after humans but not actually human themselves. They danced for men who had no doubt acquired them by less-than-legal means, and they didn't even seem to care. Not one of them looked upset or afraid.

"Why are they dressed so modestly?"

Asim laughed. "I am uncomfortable with nudity."

"That must be why you're single."

"Maybe. Are you staying?"

"No. I only have about a day to wait for you."

"We can manage it."

"I have a request."

"Yes?"

"Send everything away for me. I won't have enough time to come here again. Things are unstable, back home."

"Ship to the same address we have before?"

"Yes," she said., and then a faint smile reached her lips.

"What are you smiling about?"

"We refer to them as if they aren't human."

He laughed. "Yours rarely are, Cassie."

She stood. "Until next time."

He also vacated his seat. "Not going to stay for a bit longer?"

"I don't have time."

"You're going to see Radwan?"

"Absolutely not."

"This will be the third time you've come here without seeing him."

"And on purpose, too."

"Why don't you like him? He has no issue with

you."

"Old grudges die hard."

Marwan insisted that she have one of his cars escort her to where she needed to be and Jezebel wearily accepted. She wasn't stupid enough to allow anyone connected to him to know exactly where she was going, but a ride in the city for someone who wasn't fluent in Arabic was more than welcome.

She had the driver drop her off directly in the middle of a shopping area named West El-Balad, which was a compilation of streets lined with stores and small restaurants that served typical Egyptian food. It was always so packed with people that it would be easy for her to slip away and blend in with the crowd. One of the most remarkable things about Cairo was its citizens' ability to weave around people and avoid colliding with them without actually seeing them. Faces in crowds were empty shades of gray. They were just faint outlines in fluorescent lights that weren't worth being seen. People here only had eyes for the path toward their own destination. The way people interacted with each other here was one of the few things about Cairo that she found comparable to New York.

Jezebel slowed down as she made her way down the street, for the first time truly taking in the details of the place she had been in many a time before. She had always walked through very quickly before.

Like Manhattan, a jumbled array of taxi cabs and civilian drivers filled and jammed the streets. People were shopping on foot and walking around the cars trying to pass through, adding to the traffic congestion. Fumes emitting from exhaust pipes polluted the air and the car horns added an ear-splitting tone to the background noise typical of any busy city.

She found the lights that lit up the individual stores reminiscent of Times Square in a way. This area wasn't larger in size than the heart of Manhattan but being relatively new to the attractions around her made it seem that way. Shops lined either side of the street, each bearing a sign that seemed brighter than the next, Arabic words giving them an exotic allure that New York couldn't match. People took up space on the edge of the sidewalks selling scarves, shoes, toys, and other items for much cheaper than the stores around them.

A few minutes of walking later, Jezebel found herself at her destination. It was a clothing store with a name she was unable to pronounce. It was attached to an empty building that had never been open to the public. It was abandoned, and no one seemed to notice its existence anyway.

She could only manage to look at the sign on the door for a few moments before averting her eyes and blinking the spots clouding her vision away. It was crowded, but she pushed through the people and walked in. She took the stairs down to the lower level of the building and walked into an empty fitting room to the far left. There was no room specified for either gender; everything here was mixed.

She opened the last stall and locked the door behind her. She backed against the wall and crossed her arms, and then turned her head to the left and said, "Cassandra Rose."

Nothing happened.

She raised her voice and tried again. "Cassandra Rose."

Still, she heard nothing. She knocked on it gently and then raised her voice to say it again.

"Cassandra Rose!"

A faint voice she vaguely recognized behind the wall whispered quietly, "Leave quickly, Jezebel."

"How do you know my name?"

"It doesn't matter. Just leave."

"Why?"

"It isn't safe. Go."

"Who are you?"

"It doesn't matter! Go!"

"Why should I believe you?"

"Are you really going to argue with me when I am telling you that you are in danger?"

"I have no reason to trust you."

"Don't be an idiot! Just leave!"

Before she could make a move, someone knocked roughly on the stall door and attempted to open it.

"Occupied," she said.

She heard footsteps die away and breathed. Before she could open it to leave, another knock came, this one more violent.

"Occupied!" she repeated.

This person also walked away from her. She hesitated, and then went to the door. Just as she touched the feeble lock it was violently torn off its hinges. It crashed to the linoleum floor. Three large men stood in front of her. Two of them were extremely tall and looked as though they were all muscle and no brain. The third was shorter than she was and so pale that she doubted that he was even Egyptian. All three had similar angry expressions on their faces.

Before they could make a move someone grabbed the back of her shirt roughly and pulled her away from them. Instead of colliding with a wall, she found herself in a small, dark room. She had only been here twice before. The person who had grabbed her slammed it back into place, drowning out the shouts of the men who had been blocking her way. She pulled herself together and waited for the person who had caught her to turn.

Her eyes widened in surprise when she finally recognized who it was.

"Dad."

SEVEN

Her shocked expression melted into anger. She hadn't been prepared for this moment. She thought she would never see his face again. She had been hoping he was dead. She had never had a warm moment with him in her life. Over time the lack of emotion and caring developed into hate and bitterness. The day he left was the happiest memory she had of him.

He stepped closer to her and touched her face lightly but she slapped his hand away. He hugged her tightly, but she pushed him off and took several steps away from him. He tried to take her hands, but she pulled away immediately. He sighed and leaned back against the wall.

"Don't touch me," she said.

"I'm sorry," he replied, "I didn't mean to make you uncomfortable."

"What the hell are you doing here?" she snapped.

"I could ask you the same thing."

"What do you want from me?"

"I thought you were dead," he said.

Jezebel scoffed. "As if you care."

"Of course I care!"

"When was the last time you even saw me?"

"Just before you were kidnapped and allegedly *murdered.*"

"Just before I was kidnapped? What amount of time do you classify as 'just before?'"

"You were fourteen! You did not need a father anymore!"

"And you are sixty. You do not need a daughter anymore. Leave me the hell alone."

"When your mother died—"

"The one you murdered in cold blood?"

"I didn't kill her."

"It was your fault."

"I left because I had to."

"I don't believe you."

"Your mother and I couldn't get along. It was ruining you!"

"Yes, leaving us and starting a new life without us is less traumatic than staying and fighting with her."

"Yes, it is. You were always on her side anyway."

"I deserved it then."

"That isn't my point."

"You are not innocent. Don't absolve yourself."

"You are too old to be fighting about this with me, Belle."

"Do not call me that."

"I'm sorry."

She shook her head and turned away to find an exit. She was standing on a narrow wooden platform with no furniture of any kind. Behind her was an unsteady staircase that led down somewhere into deep darkness. She took a few steps toward them, but he caught her arm and turned her back to him. She wrenched herself from his grasp and moved further away.

"Listen to me," he said.

"Why? I will never forgive you."

"I don't care. How did you get into this business? *Why* did you get into this business?"

"Like father, like daughter."

"I quit after I lost you."

"Then why are you here?"

"I'm looking for you!"

"You knew where to find me. You did not have to come all the way to Egypt for this audacious and pseudo-heartfelt reunion you claim you wanted. So tell me what the hell you're really doing here."

He avoided the question. "How did you get out? That isn't supposed to be possible."

Jezebel ignored him and looked around, again. She had been there twice before, and neither time was she hunted by any number of strangers. Both times were just ten-minute meetings with a man she detested.

"Jezebel," he said.

She turned back to her father whose face suddenly seemed so old. His once raven-colored hair had faded into weak strands of gray, thinning ever-so-greatly from the back of his neck to his nose. Deep lines had etched themselves into his forehead and cheeks. Though he had always had more color than she, his skin had faded into a frosted pastel. He was paler than any ghost she had ever seen. His brown eyes seemed smaller, sadder, and significantly emptier than she remembered. The flame in his eyes that she inherited was dead, and it was replaced with a bleak deadness. He looked terrible, but her hatred for him ran deeper than any sympathy she may have once been able to muster. She felt nothing.

"I owe you no answers."

"I missed you."

"Liar."

"Do you want me to apologize?"

"I want you to tell me what the hell you're doing

here, because no apology can erase what you did."

"I just wanted to protect you. Go home."

"And you waited until I came all the way to Cairo and put myself in danger before bothering to make an appearance."

"I can't just see you in New York, and you wouldn't have listened to me anyway."

"How did you know I was taken?"

"The news reached me after I was told you were killed."

"That wasn't my question."

"It doesn't matter. What matters is that I want you safe."

"Too late."

"It's never too late. Radwan sold this place to someone else just a few weeks ago and he's no longer here. Go home."

"No," she said.

Just as his thin lips parted to say another word a gunshot tore through the silence. Before she could manage to blink twice a bullet pierced through her father's chest. As his body began to fall toward the floor, she couldn't manage to tear her gaze away as the light slowly left his eyes. Time seemed to stop, and nothing in the world was sharper than the image of her paternal bloodline becoming entirely obsolete. She wasn't hurt by this death; he had been dead to her for years.

Jezebel pulled herself together, and then hurled herself into the darkness that swallowed the stairwell. She ran down the stairs hearing the wood under her protest under the impact of her weight. There was no banister, making the trip down even more unsafe. She couldn't tell where the stairs would end, and the lack of a wall on either side of her made it impossible for her to lean on anything. She couldn't see anything that was around her.

She reached the bottom of the stairwell and stumbled, twisting her ankle in the process. She ignored the pain and turned back to the seemingly endless darkness. She mentally prepared herself for death and vaguely wondered if Amir and Hanem would ever find out what had happened to her. She suddenly couldn't remember how the hell she had gotten out before. Everything was unclear.

She could hear no one behind her, but this neither slowed her down nor comforted her. She tripped over a piece of wood and fell over, her shoulder and head hitting the cement hard. She lay there for a few seconds before pulling herself up and taking off again, this time a little slower and with her arms outstretched. It was colder now. The pain in the back of her head was growing, and she struggled to ignore it. Memories began flashing through her mind and she couldn't force them out.

"Wake up!" she shouted. "Wake up, please!"

A fair-haired woman of small body and pale skin had collapsed onto a tile floor. She refused to respond to a girl of fourteen, whose voice had begun to crack, and strength begun to wean. The girl was on her knees, her face burrowed into the woman's stomach and gripping the thin white blouse that seemed too crisp and clean to be anywhere near this lifeless body. She was too shocked to cry, and her guilt was holding her from breathing steadily.

Lying in the woman's limp hand was an empty glass bottle. What was left of its red, liquid content had spilled onto the floor. Her eyes were opened and her mouth was closed. Her long hair was sprawled in immaculate curls all around her. Blood trickled from the corner where her lips met and slid across her right cheek onto the floor.

Jezebel slammed into a metal door and stumbled back. After a few seconds of disorientation she blinked and felt for a handle, but nothing was there. It was just a smooth block of metal that didn't budge upon contact. She burrowed her nails in the cracks to claw it open, but it remained perfectly intact. She tried for several more seconds, and then felt one of her nails break. Her finger started bleeding and she flinched, but she didn't stop.

She let go of the attempt to pry it open and felt around for something else higher on the wall. She pushed herself up onto the tips of her toes to find some kind of latch, and her fingers finally grazed a deadbolt. She mustered all of her strength to slide it open, the flesh under her broken nail burning and bleeding all over it.

After a minute's tremendous effort it slid open a small hole just big enough to fit. She fell to her knees and crawled through it, still completely blind. She was moving slower now, trying not to harm another part of her body. She reached another wall, and against it were metal bars neatly stacked over each other like a ladder. She stood and took the first step, but the one above it was so high that it took her a few seconds to place her foot on it and lift herself up.

The consecutive steps were not as high, and she climbed up slowly. She felt metal double doors above her that were slanted, like the door to a basement. She held onto the ladder with one arm and pushed it up with all her might. She climbed out and found herself in the heart of the city again. She stood and closed the doors, finally pausing to take a breath.

Again, she was in the midst of a thick crowd, standing right in front of the abandoned building. People didn't even seem fazed by her, and she felt disoriented. She knew exactly where she was: back in West El-

Balad, drowned in bright lights and blinded by the mass of faces she couldn't recognize. She was being shoved from right to left as the people around her hurried along. She felt deaf to the loud noises that surrounded her. It was as though she were frozen in time while the rest of the world kept marching on.

Some indiscernible amount of time later she pulled herself together and moved. She wasn't sure in which direction she was going, but she didn't stop to think about it. Her only thought consisted of a screaming voice in her suddenly very empty head telling her to get away. Her memories were gone. She was just in a daze.

She hailed a taxi and got in, fumbling to find words.

"Airport," she said.

"You okay?" he asked.

She took deep breaths and nodded. "Go."

He looked uncomfortable but he pulled off in silence. As the trip went on Jezebel's shock wore off, and she was able to think more clearly. She leaned her head back and closed her eyes, breathing in the night air. She moved her face closer to the window and let the air hit her face. Her anxiety calmed but she stayed silent for the rest of the ride.

The driver arrived at their intended destination, and she paid him and vacated the vehicle. She watched him drive away in silence and then entered the airport, mindlessly finding a ticket counter and moving her ticket to the District of Columbia to the earliest possible time. She didn't stop to think about the mess she had left behind.

As soon as she was on the plane she took a pill and forced herself to sleep.

EIGHT

The white sand that embraced her feet was unusually warm for half past midnight. The salt-clad air laid a thin coat of bitterness on her lips, compelling her to tear at them with her teeth. The wind was strong, but silent; her thin, deep-blue skirt billowed around her threatening to expose some body part or other. As uncomfortable as she generally was with nudity she made no move to stop it. In fact, she made no attempt to move at all. She was almost paralyzed by the sight before her. It was one of the few places in which violence and peace wove themselves together so beautifully.

She remembered sitting in the glorified dirt cupping her hands and allowing the grains to seep through her fingers. She had never attempted to create anything artistic with it. She knew it would be a wasted effort, but still she would play with it for hours, getting lost in the crashing waves of ink that made up the sea. She never physically stepped into the water; imagination had always been enough.

Presently, Jezebel stood just beyond the wet area

still resistant to being touched by the water, even so many years later. A royal blue sky littered with glistening white diamonds had begun to disappear behind dark clouds. A crescent moon struggled to make its presence known in the night, but it was losing to the puffs of smoke floating just beyond it. Despite the cold and darkness it was serene. No storms were coming. The sky was just in a surly mood. It was much less sinister than it had been the last time she had come here.

The sea salt invaded her pores and enflamed her face. She stood on the edge of a cliff in almost total darkness, aside from the full moon that shined all too ominously in the midst of black clouds. Lightning cracked over the water, and it took great deal of effort to keep from jumping out of her skin every time. No rain fell, but the bitter cold air crashed into her body from all directions. Her hands were shaking, and shivers ran up and down her spine.

The wind moaned in the night, the air pressure doing a harsh number on her eardrums. The cliff was reminiscent of a blackened tongue unrolled to its furthest extent to taunt all that stood atop it. Despite only being about halfway up the rock wall, it was attached to, the face of the sea was miles below it. The drop of a coin would cause severe damage from here. A drop of a person would be fatal.

She had never been altophobic and had always loved the ocean, but the sight of the waves reaching heights she had never before witnessed and the lack of a barrier between her and a fall that would surely end in a gruesome death increased her heart rate and brought her to the threshold of panic. She tried to keep her intake of breath at a normal level, but it wasn't working. She could do no more than keep her hyperventilation silent.

However, her fear was insignificant compared to the terror reflected on the face of the man to her right. He was on his knees, far closer to the edge than she, eyes closed, skin pale, and breathing irregular. The dark curls that usually stood at odd ends were matted onto his head by his own sweat. There were deep gashes across his left cheek that had been left uncleaned long enough to fester.

He was mumbling something to himself on a continuous loop, no noise actually coming out of him. His hands were bound so tightly behind his back that the ropes tore into his wrists, his skin chafing and tearing against them. She pitied him. He had done nothing to deserve this.

Two of the other figures behind her moved to stand on either side of him, knocking into her in the process. She stumbled, and her heart jumped into her throat as she fell. His jaw connected with the rock she stood on and her teeth closed harshly on her tongue. She missed a plunge to her death by mere inches. Pain shot through her as the taste of blood filled her mouth. She spat out the liquid, and the third man on the ledge gripped her arm and pulled her to her feet gently.

She shot him a confused look that he didn't turn to see, and then reverted her attention to the man they had made the trip for. The twin brothers who had pushed her were wielding daggers that flashed in the moonlight. They thrust the blades into his stomach, and then dragged them across his abdomen. The man's body pulsed, but he didn't make a sound. They watched blood spurt from the wounds for a few seconds, and then caught his arms and hurled him over the cliff.

She took a few steps forward to bring herself just close enough to the edge to watch him fall. His body shot toward the raging sea like a lightning bolt. His figure grew fainter as he raced toward the bottom, until the night swallowed him, and he existed no more.

"Miss Jezebel White," a voice to her right said and she involuntarily blinked the scene away.

There was no need for her to look in order to know what, or rather who, had graced her with his presence. She turned to him and almost smiled faintly. It had been years.

A dark-haired and fairly built man with skin the color of a caramel apple had appeared by her side. He was remarkably tall, towering over her and able to see over her head with ease. He wore a bright, kind smile that never seemed to disappear. He wasn't nearly as angelic as he seemed to be, but he was still a better man than she.

He was over-dressed for a meeting on a beach. He wore an expensive black pin-striped suit and suede shoes. She had never seen him wear the same outfit more than once; he considered it a poor man's choice to repeat an outfit. He would never admit it but he had something of an inferiority complex that created a need to out-style everyone around him. He was neither racist nor a bigot, but he was not blind to color.

She had always been a special case. There was nothing that she could say that he would take offense to. She could be abrasive in nature at times, but there was no bigotry behind her words.

Though she hadn't heard him coming, she wasn't fazed. She kept her eyes fixed on the water and waited for him to speak again. She was too tired to make polite conversation.

"I have what you asked me for," he said.

"That was fast."

"I did my best." He handed her a black leather briefcase. Her fingers closed around it and she let her arm drop to her side limply.

"You'll be shocked when you open that briefcase."

"You know that it's hard to shock me, Lionel."

"First time for everything, Jezebel."

She looked down at the wet area that she was carefully avoiding. "Not everything."

"Why are we meeting here?"

She didn't respond. She kept her gaze on the line that separated her from the water. He crossed his arms impatiently, eyes darting between her and the crashing waves nervously. This tall, intimidating man was terrified of the ocean and he couldn't swim. He would always mask his nervousness with humor, but she had known him for too long to buy into the illusion.

"Jezebel."

She took one step onto the wet sand and diverted her gaze to the water. "Ernest Hemingway once described the sea as though it were a living, breathing woman."

"That's a nautical reference. Sailors refer to their boats and the open water as if they're females."

"Yes, but it was more than just colloquial terminology, the way he wrote about it."

"How so?"

"The sea was loved, hated, and fought. She could give great favors and just as often destroy everything. She would do wicked things because she couldn't help it. Despite how terrible she was, how treacherous she had a tendency to be, they loved her. They loved the sea."

"I don't understand why that's significant."

"I didn't expect you to."

He rolled his eyes and changed the subject. "You know what I find very interesting?"

"You're fully aware that I don't care."

"That rhymed."

"Don't be annoying, Lionel."

"Make me."

"I'm going to throw something at you."

"You don't scare me, Jezebel White."

"I could hurt you."

He laughed. "You're half my size."

"You are so dramatic."

"Just pushing your buttons."

"I'll push you in the water."

"I don't care."

"Oh, I'm sure."

"I'm an adult. A little water doesn't scare me."

"Step in, then."

"I won't ruin these shoes just to prove myself to you."

"Take one step if you're so brave."

"You can't give me orders."

"It looks like I just did."

"Stop it. Right now."

"You can't tell me what to do. I'm not a little kid anymore."

"You still act like one."

"You think I won't hurt you?"

"No, you won't."

"You're delusional."

"I resent that."

"Is there any end to this conversation in sight?"

"Why do you use a different name on every continent you travel to but practice with your real name at home? Wouldn't it be more dangerous to be yourself in New York?"

"It's easier this way."

"I don't get it."

"Well, that's because you're an idiot."

"You know damn well that there was never an infiltration in your division, Jezebel."

"And you know all this because you're my personal

confidant?"

"I used to be."

"Things change."

"What the hell are you doing here?"

"Stay out of it."

"Why are you making Hanem do all that work for nothing?"

"To distract him."

"From?"

"Someone is trying to frame me, Lionel."

"How do you know this?"

"Athena Elias."

"Bugsy killed her for revenge. I thought you knew that."

"Athena Elias was not drugging Bugsy Marcel's sister. She was an addict herself."

"Addicts can be dealers, too."

"I know that, but this is different. She is not a drug dealer. She may not be innocent of all crime in general, but I'm sure that she was not who she was portrayed to be."

"You think he was lying?"

"Elias was nothing more than a decoy that had been planted in my office as a trap, and I took the bait."

"Do you remember her file?"

"It wasn't a file. I saw her attacking a little girl in a park, and I don't think it was an accident that I ended up witnessing that exact moment. I forgot about the incident until just a few days ago."

"She wasn't one of your patients?"

"No. Her file appeared in my records. I have never seen her in that capacity. I didn't remember where I found her until I met with Bugsy and heard his side of the story."

"Yet you claim you forget nothing."

"This isn't funny, Lionel."

"Sorry. What are you going to do with Bugsy?"

"Plant clear evidence that he murdered Athena Elias to protect his sister. She is the only woman in his life who can willingly spend time with him without causing him severe pain, and for questionable reasons. I doubt that anyone likes him enough to vouch for him."

"What about Jules?"

"He won't want to cross me."

"Marcel's career will be over."

"I don't care. I'll be a mockery if I do any less, and it isn't as if he doesn't deserve to rot in jail for the rest of his miserable life. I'm not framing him. He is not an innocent man."

"And you are not an innocent woman."

"Nor have I ever pretended to be."

"You're just saving face."

"I'm saving my business."

"And now you're trying to find out who is trying to frame you?"

"No. Now, I'm trying to meet my quotas without giving anyone a chance to ruin my reputation by connecting me to any criminal activity. One detective has already put a target on my back."

"So he says."

She looked at him. "So he says?"

"Don't take too long to read that file. You haven't got the time."

"I asked you to fill a quota, not stalk someone who is already doing his best to put me behind bars."

"I did what you asked me to do. I just did a little bit more."

"I didn't ask you to."

"I don't need your permission."

"I don't need you to take care of me."

"I'll do what I want."

"You are way too confident that I wouldn't hurt

you."

"You wouldn't."

"And why's that?"

"Because you love me."

She rolled her eyes. "Go away, Lionel."

"But I want to spend time with you."

"Goodbye."

"Fine."

He immediately turned and made his way to wherever he had come from and she turned back to the water. She stood there for several long minutes, mind completely blank. She had the sudden urge to sing loudly, even though she didn't have the most decent of voices.

"So gentle could the changes be, if it were I, myself, and the sea."

The wind lifted the words from her lips and gently carried them out over the water, losing them in the sound of crashing waves.

Just as she turned to leave something hard connected with her skull and she collapsed into the sand.

Jezebel opened her eyes groggily and was momentarily dazed and confused. She could not for the life of her recognize her surroundings. Her memory was a total blur. She didn't know how she had gotten herself into a bed. The light was far too bright, and burned her eyes the moment she snapped them open. The room was cold, and though she was covered in thick blankets, she shivered.

She finally pulled herself together and sat up. She felt as though a train had run over her body. The idea of moving became increasingly unattractive by the second. She rubbed her eyes violently to help wake herself up, and then finally, her brain registered where she was.

She was in her own bedroom, dressed in the exact clothes she had been wearing before someone had knocked her unconscious. There was no sign of forced entry; everything was exactly where it should have been. It seemed like someone had actually cleaned the room.

Jezebel stumbled out of the bed and noticed the leather bag Lionel had given her sitting on the bedside table. She opened it and found many documents held together with a paperclip. It would be foolish to accept any of it as truth now. Whoever had attacked her had wanted something, and whatever he had left was either unimportant or fabrications to mislead her and she had a nagging feeling that she wouldn't be able to ask Lionel for help. Something had happened.

It was not the attack on her that made her anxious. She was always prepared for someone to assault her in some way. She had many enemies. She had survived and that was all that mattered. It was something else. She couldn't quite place it; or rather, she wasn't ready to place it. She would keep the feeling at bay for as long as possible, avoiding reality until she couldn't anymore.

She put the papers back in the bag and went to clean up. She gathered clothes from her dresser and stepped into the shower. She turned the water on and stood stoically under the circular panel the hung above her head. She felt faint, almost detached from her body. She stared at the tiled wall in front of her without really seeing it, afraid to finish and be forced to step back into a reality she knew that she wasn't ready for. Something outside was waiting to knock her cleanly off her feet. She breathed deeply as the water slid down her skin like incandescent raindrops.

Her eyes watered, and tears made their way down her cheeks. She didn't know yet why there was an unshakeable ache in her chest. Her heart was slowly breaking, and a piece of it disappeared to a place outside of her body.

Her mother laid her down in her bed and sat on the edge. She took her hand and rubbed it gently, coaxing the little girl's fear and anxiety out of her mind. Her hands were unstable and frail, but she didn't falter. Another child entered the room, but he stood by the bed in silence, waiting for the woman to ease his fears as well. She brushed his cheek with her hand and gave him a simple, kind smile. She pulled him into her lap and rested her chin on his head.

She began to sing to them softly, her voice so soothing that it kept the nightmares away.

'When you fall asleep
And the Sandman comes to pull you under
If moments pass
And you're all alone
Lost and confused
And can't find your way home
Your eyes are too heavy
To come back and escape
You went too far
You had made a mistake
If you are lost inside the dreams
And the nightmares come, as loud as thunder
Find us there to catch the tears
To pull you out when you're too far gone
You'll find yourself inside our arms
Tell me have you been waiting long?
And when day comes
If I'm dead and gone
Find your comfort in this song
Think of me and then you'll say
She's still here, with me, today'

She turned off the water and stepped back out into the cold world. She dried herself and dressed in a simple, black dress. She caught a glimpse of her face in the mirror. The girl in it looked so fragile. It was like a mere huff and a puff could blow her down. She was just a speck in the universe, a drop in an ocean, and she didn't matter at all.

Her feet carried her to her office, where Hanem sat silently. She didn't bother to sit behind her desk. She stopped in front of him, waiting. He stood and looked down at her, eyes dim and expression dark.

She waited in silence for him to say something, but he was struggling to find a gentle way to tell her the truth. He knew that she didn't truly need him to say it out loud, but he had to.

"Something's happened," he said.

She swallowed and took a deep breath. Her eyes watered but she couldn't blink it away. A single tear fell from her right eye, falling across her face and dripping from her chin. She didn't bother to wipe it.

"Lionel?" she asked.

"I'm sorry, Jezebel."

NINE

Jezebel stood in a dimly lit room, looking at a mahogany casket that was shut tightly. She sat in the chair next to it not sure what to do. She had very little time left. The service would start in just a few minutes. She touched it gently, and a feeling of terrible guilt washed over her. She was the reason it was here, the reason he was in it, the reason this day was so bleak.

Only Hanem and Amir stood with her, both in black suits and standing on either side of her. Neither had ever seen her look so empty before.

She gathered her strength and opened the lid, but immediately dropped it when she saw the body. Amir caught it before it slammed and closed it gently. He looked at her, and she motioned for him to reopen it. He lifted the lid again and propped it up for her.

Lionel lay in the box, arms resting at his sides and eyes closed. His skin was covered in scars, but aside from this, he could have easily been sleeping. She touched his face, but it was so cold that she moved her hand away quickly. He had always been so warm. In all of their time together, he would hold her hands to spread his warmth to her whenever she was cold. He had always taken care of her as much as he could, and how little had she appreciated it.

Amir stood next to her silently, trying to comfort her without speaking. She wasn't ready to talk.

"You can go, Hanem."

"Is there anything you want me to do?" he asked.

"No."

"Alright."

He left, but Amir stayed.

"I don't need you, Amir," she said.

"I know."

"You are not special."

"I know."

"I can take care of myself."

"I know."

"Get out."

"I am not here for emotional support. I'm here because it is my job to be where you are."

"I'm safe."

"After this murder, we need to heighten your security for some time. It doesn't have to be me, but someone should be with you wherever you are until we figure out what's going on."

"I don't need your protection."

"You need a security detail. After the funeral, pick someone else."

"You aren't going to fight me on this?"

"No."

She didn't say anything, and he didn't break the silence. They sat together, her looking at the coffin and him looking at her.

"My father died," she said.

"I didn't know you were still in contact with him," Amir said.

"I wasn't."

"How did you find out?"

She ignored the question. "Hanem once asked me if I was starting to enjoy this, and I was shocked by the question. How could anyone enjoy something so evil? I've always known deep down that it wasn't true, but I had myself convinced that what I'm doing is almost noble. I'm replacing innocent people with others who deserve punishment. I'm saving souls who I find innocent and damning the wicked to the bowels of hell. Oh, my bleeding, dramatic heart. I'm as close to god as a woman could possibly be. It's pathetic."

"You aren't as much a villain as you paint yourself to be."

And just like that, she burst into tears. He pulled her into a hug, and she didn't pull away. She just kept sobbing. She couldn't control it. Years of suppressed emotion spilled out of her onto his shirt, and she didn't even try to pull herself together. She was crying so hard that she couldn't regulate her breathing. She was hyperventilating and working herself into a massive panic attack. Amir was talking but she couldn't hear him. Walls were closing in on her and she felt suffocated. She was in danger of passing out but she didn't care.

Ten minutes went by and she finally calmed down. She pulled away from him and sat up in her chair. She looked back at the box. The most painful of it all was that she was sure he had completely forgiven her for it.

She had ruined someone who had truly loved her.

Again.

"My father was murdered in cold blood before my eyes, and I felt nothing," she said. "I wasn't sad, or angry, or vengeful. Actually, at this very moment, a significant part of me is happy that he is dead. It gives me great comfort that I will never have to see his face again. What kind of person—normal person—could feel that way about her own father?"

"He was a terrible father. You can't blame yourself for that."

"But I am so much like him."

"You are nothing like him!"

"I took after him in many ways. I'm selfish, self-centered, cruel, cold, dead, dark and—"

"You're trying to manipulate a system to prevent the torture of innocent people! That is a noble act!"

"A noble act is working to prevent the system altogether."

"That's impossible."

"Only because I have always been too selfish and afraid for my own well-being to take a chance."

"You wouldn't succeed anyway."

"You don't know that."

"Being selfless is difficult."

"Being human is not."

A few minutes of silence later, Hanem entered the room and gently touched her shoulder.

"It's time," he said.

"Do you need another moment?" Amir asked her.

She shook her head and stepped away. Amir closed the casket. He, along with Hanem and two other men, lifted it together. She watched them take it out to the hearse parked outside of the funeral home. They loaded it in and closed the doors. Amir touched her arm and led her to his car, Hanem close behind. Hanem held the passenger door open for her, and she got in.

Amir and Hanem joined her inside the car, and then Amir pulled out of the parking lot. He drove directly behind the hearse in silence and carefully took her hand. Her better judgment berated her for not moving away, but she was too numb to listen. Instead, she turned her head toward the window and watched everything fly by. Hanem didn't comment.

They pulled into the graveyard, but she didn't step out of the car. Amir and Hanem went to place the casket in its rightful place, and she just watched them. The sun was too bright, the air too clear, the birds far too happy to be appropriate for this occasion. She couldn't seem to get out of her seat. She had forgotten how to move her legs.

Amir got into the driver's seat again and waited, but she didn't say anything or look his way.

"Whenever you're ready," he said.

"So many people are here to witness this."

"Lionel was loved."

"He deserved it."

"Yes, he did."

She looked at him. "Don't die before me."

"I'm not going anywhere."

She looked back at the people who were waiting outside. "The funeral should have started by now."

"You decide when it starts."

"They've all already sat down."

"Let them wait."

"I've kept them too long."

She hesitated, and then said, "Amir."

"You don't have to."

"Okay."

She stepped out of the car and walked through the crowd. She took the seat that had been saved for her at the front, and Amir stood next to her. Hanem was standing with Adel in the back, watching everyone carefully. Adel was focusing on the crowd, and Hanem was watching their surrounding area. Five other men were sitting in seats toward the middle, blending in with the crowd.

A pastor stood at the head and started talking, but she couldn't hear him. Her mind had wandered to memories she hadn't forgotten. She thought of the good times and the bad. She thought of all the moments they once had together that meant the world to her.

"Jezebel," Amir said.

The pastor had finished speaking, and all eyes were on her. She walked to the head of the casket and looked around at all the faces that had come to see him off. There were not many that she recognized. Lionel had many friends. He was kind and compassionate, and few people disliked him.

"Lionel Madison was one of the most phenomenal people I have ever known," she began. "There's nothing I can say today that could ever describe well enough how wonderful he was. He was gentle, and though he was not naïve he was willing to give second chances. His judgment of people was excellent. He wasn't easily fooled, and it was difficult to hate him."

She looked at all of the people she had never taken the time to meet. They seemed genuinely upset. They were of all different races, ethnicities, and social class. There wasn't an ounce of bigotry in this man's heart.

"He gave me everything in his power to give. He never held me back. He did his best to protect me. He took care of me for the majority of my life, until I grew older and began to shut him out. Even when I treated him like he meant very little to me, he did what was best for me before even thinking of himself. I wish that I could have been given the chance to show him how much I appreciated it.

"Lionel was by no means a saint. He had a very difficult time conforming to morality. He could be cruel just as easily as he could be kind. He made mistakes that he didn't try to correct. He rarely felt guilty for anything he did. He regularly did and said things that were ridiculously inappropriate, and he could be effortlessly ruthless when the situation demanded it. Yet still, he was also somehow caring, loyal, and loved, and the world will sorely miss him. I know I will."

"Give that back!" she yelled at a boy who was no less than five inches taller than her.

He grinned. "Make me."

He ran away, and she shot after him. They ran into the sea of trees that haunted the town just as the sun made its exit from the sky. She found herself inside a darkness that was only thinly penetrated by the feeble light of the crescent moon that hung above her. An unnerving stillness had fallen over the forest. The animals she had seen just moments before disappeared into their respective havens, clinging to a safety she would never find here.

The silence was deafening. She had heard nothing louder than the sudden lack of noise that brought all impending action in the forest to a muted crashing halt. She didn't move. She was afraid that any sound she made would ring out across the ominous compilation of trees and draw attention to her.

She heard a twig snap behind her and immediately shut her eyes. Nothing good would come of knowing what was about to attack her. She waited, taking care to remain as still as possible, but no other noise reached her ears. She swallowed and opened her eyes, but as soon as her lids parted, she saw another pair of black pupils not two inches from her face.

She stumbled back and fell over, twisting her ankle in the process. Almost as quickly as they had appeared, the eyes vanished. She saw nothing but darkness again. Moments later, a shrill scream pierced the air. The sound was so high-pitched that she was unsure if it had even been human. The screaming was continuous, and it only seemed to grow louder with every passing second.

Just as she had managed to gain balance on her aching foot, the scream was accompanied by the sound *of something crashing to the ground. So strong was the impact that the earth beneath her shook, forcing her to fall to her knees. She heard a howl in the distance, and someone—or something—was slamming what sounded like a thick bar of metal against a tree. The slamming steadily grew louder. The being responsible was moving in her direction.*

She heard a soft, mirthless snickering to her left—this sound also playing on a continuous loop without pause—joining the screaming in perfect mismatched harmony that drilled holes into her ears. The person assaulting the trees had come so close that she could hear the footsteps, as well as an unidentifiable humming.

Someone grabbed her and pulled her to her feet. Just before she screamed, a hand covered her mouth. Her breathing came in short, painful gasps, and her heart beat so hard that it could be felt through her shirt.

"Quiet," the person said, and her panic decreased when she recognized his voice. He let go of her mouth and held her face gently. "Nothing bad happens in Mathews County. Nothing bad ever happens in Mathews County."

The slamming, the screaming, and the laughing suddenly stopped. They fell into complete silence once more.

"We're okay," he said.

As soon as he said it, all three sounds erupted in unison around them. She nearly fell over, but he caught her. He pushed her behind him and faced the direction of the approaching assailant, shielding her body with his. He was left defenseless.

The humming resumed just as the screaming ceased, and the person approaching them began to hit the trees with greater force. The metal connected with the bark almost melodically, like violent church bells on a cold Christmas night. The tune was soft and sad, as if it were made to play at a wake or funeral.

Seconds later, the bat fell to the ground, and they heard people laughing. A group of kids came out of the shadows.

"Babies," one of them said.

The boy who had been protecting her promptly balled his hands into fists and punched one of the mocking children square in the face. The child stumbled back and fell. The rest of them ran away.

She took a deep breath and closed her eyes.

"And I loved him very, very much. I wish I had managed to tell him that enough when I had the chance. May he rest in peace."

They began to lower him into the ground, and she watched him go. The piece of her heart that had earlier escaped her had found its final resting place in the ground; with the man she had stopped visiting after she had turned sixteen.

"So, you just kill people and then facilitate their burials," she heard a voice to her left say.

She didn't turn to him, but she said, "You are not welcome here. Please, just leave."

"This isn't private property. You can't kick me out."

"You are so disgusting that you would disrespect the dead while the dirt on his grave is still fresh?"

"This is just another act to cover up what you've done, isn't it?"

"You don't know what the hell you're talking about."

"Was he another one of your lovers, Morticia?"

She turned her angry gaze on him, her eyes unwillingly filling with tears. "You will regret making a mockery of my brother's funeral. I will not forget this, and people who leave a mark in my memory always come to hate me in ways they had never thought possible."

Before the casket had even reached the bottom, she had walked away. She got into Amir's car, turned on the engine and drove away alone. Amir could find his own way back. No one came looking for her for the rest of the day. She spent it sitting by herself in her office, the shades drawn and her head on her desk as she shamed herself to death.

<u>TEN</u>

The station was loud and overcrowded. People were rushing around, taking papers to different desks, walking in and out in a frenzy. It was a large room with nine desks spread about in no particular order, and a copy machine was against a wall to the left. There was a line of people waiting to use it, all of them talking to each other, some laughing and others having more serious conversations. There was nothing special about it that was worth noting.

She was seated in an uncomfortable plastic chair by an unstable wooden desk. It seemed as if it could carry no more than a glass of water and a paperback book. She sat quietly, watching people run around with myriad papers, and hearing them have many loud and mindless conversations. It all melted into one unclear combination of noise that would cause a headache for any newcomer who stayed too long. Someone was playing the same song over and over, making her want to turn around and snap at him. The song itself was just a chaotic mess of instrumental noise that had no words.

The room was unreasonably hot. The number of

people inside emitted enough body heat to ignite Satan's fireplace. Everyone around her didn't seem to notice at all. They were all wearing heavy sweaters and jackets. No one seemed perturbed by the room's temperature at all.

A pale, old man sat at the desk in front of her, giving her an artificial smile. He folded his wrinkled, spotted hands on the table in front of him and leaned toward her, waiting for her to speak first. She offered him a smile that was as—if not more—insincere as his, letting him sit uncomfortably under her intense gaze until he broke the silence himself.

"Did you want something?" he condescended.

"No, I'm here for no reason at all."

The comment annoyed him. "What can I do for you?"

"You can bring me someone else to talk to."

He looked highly affronted by the comment. "Who the hell do you think you are?"

"Doesn't matter. I would like to talk to Detective Wilson."

"This is not a restaurant. You will not give me orders."

"Would it help if I said please?"

"Yes."

"Please, then."

"Who are you?"

"Go get him, and he can tell you himself."

"I'm not a messenger."

"You are today."

"Get out."

"I haven't done anything for you to forcibly remove me."

"I can do what I want."

"I doubt that."

"This is a private department."

She ignored him and stood up. She looked around the small, frazzled room, searching for the one reason she had reluctantly brought herself to a police precinct by choice. Despite the cramped nature of the room, Jezebel couldn't find him anywhere in sight.

"Jezebel," someone behind her said.

She turned around, and there was the towering figure that was Detective Asher Wilson. He looked uncomfortable at the sight of her, for some reason. He composed himself and crossed his arms.

"Hello," she said.

"Let's go outside," he said.

She followed him to the door, but they didn't leave the building.

"What do you want?" he asked.

She gave him the file in her hand and said, "Don't say I never did anything for you."

She turned and left without another word. The black, tinted car she had come in was waiting for her by the precinct door. She took her seat in the back, but before the door was closed, Wilson hopped in next to her.

"What do you want?" she asked.

"Why are you giving me this?" he asked.

"This is the man who murdered Athena Elias."

"Why are you helping me?"

"I am not helping you."

"You could have given this to anyone else."

"Why don't you want it?"

"I didn't say that."

"I want you out of my life. You're a nuisance, and if I don't prove to you that I am innocent of all the crimes you're convinced I'm guilty of, you will continue to be a nuisance until the day you die."

"You assume I'll die first?"

"I have a better life insurance policy than you do."

"Why should I believe any of this?"

"None of the evidence I gave you is circumstantial. These are facts that you can check yourself. I don't expect you to believe me."

"Just yesterday, you were threatening me at your brother's funeral, and now you're giving me evidence to solve a murder case?"

"Yes."

"Give me a reason."

"I decided that the only way to honor that threat is to ruin your investigation. I can just give those documents to someone else, if you don't want them."

"There has to be more than this."

"I doubt your boss will see it that way. Get out of my car."

He stepped out, but before the car pulled off into the street, he said, "This isn't over."

"I didn't think it would be, Detective Shepherd."

"Excuse me?"

"Don't underestimate me. It'll hurt more when you lose."

She motioned for the driver to move and he stood in the middle of the street, watching her get away.

Not twenty minutes after she had taken a seat at her desk, Wilson charged in. He looked angrier than a bull who'd just seen red. He leaned on her desk with closed fists and attempted to give her an intimidating look, but the scowl he wore was laced with building panic. She could see it in the lines of his face, in the furrow of his brow. He was terrified of what she could do to him.

"I will not be blackmailed."

"Blackmail? Whatever do you mean?"

"I'm not. I just wonder if your fellow police officers are aware that you aren't who you say you are."

"What do you want?"

"I want information."

"I will not become an informant."

"I'm not interested in your investigation. I'm not guilty of what you're trying to charge me with. I'm going to offer you a deal, and I would strongly recommend that you accept it."

"Are you implying that I have no choice?"

"Take it however you want to take it."

"Spare me the pleasantries."

"Brushing up on our vocabulary, are we?"

"Tell me what you want."

"You want to solve this case and convince your fellow police officers that you are not the failure they know you are."

"Make your point."

"I'll help you crack it."

"I thought you gave me all the evidence I need."

"Are you content with just throwing Marcel in jail?"

He paused, and then asked, "What do you want in return?"

"We'll see."

"I don't work for you."

"You do now."

He gritted his teeth angrily but didn't respond.

"The first thing you will do is find every single thing there is to know about my father," Jezebel said.

"How can I be sure that I can trust you?"

"You cannot. You should not. You never will. You're right to be afraid of me."

"I am not afraid of you."

"I'm sure."

"Why are you asking me?"

"Because even though I know you are a complete idiot you might still be useful to me."

"Stop talking down to me."

"I don't take orders."

"I'll do it, but I won't be your lackey. You will

respect me at all times."

"No."

"Yes."

"Your beliefs, desires, and demands, are irrelevant. I don't compromise. I don't listen. I don't care. Make your decision. You have two days to give me what I want, beginning with where he was for the entirety of my adolescence."

"How old are you?"

"We're done here."

He turned and stalked out. Hanem walked in and set the briefcase that she had woken up with on a chair. He pulled out its contents and looked through each paper carefully.

"Is all of this true?" he asked.

"Yes," Jezebel said. "Which only complicates this situation."

Amir walked into the room holding a sandwich and water. He set them down in front of her.

"Eat," he said.

"I ate."

"Not enough."

"I'm fine."

"Just eat, Jezebel."

"Fine."

He stepped back and waited.

"Are you going to stand there until I eat it?"

"Yes."

"Why are you really here, Amir?"

"I need a reason?"

"Yes."

"You haven't eaten."

"You look angry."

"I'm not."

"Don't treat me like I'm fragile just because my brother is gone. Be a man and tell me what's wrong."

He crossed his arms. "How can you not expect me to be upset? You disappeared without a word. You told Hanem everything, but you ignored me. I didn't matter at all to you."

"You would have followed me. I'm an adult. I do not need you to take care of me."

"Tell me where you went."

"Not right now."

"Then tell me why that detective was here just now."

"This isn't the time to talk about it. Accept that or leave."

"I'm tired of being ignored."

"I don't owe you anything, Amir. Go do what I hired you to do."

"I'm trying. You won't let me."

"Your job isn't to follow me around. You're starting to slip on your other responsibilities because you're constantly only focused on where I am and what I'm doing."

"Don't make it seem like I'm stalking you. I'm supposed to protect you. You pay me to do that, and I do it well when you let me."

"You're neglecting other aspects of your job."

"I do what I'm supposed to do. I used to guard you just the same before you were thrown into this situation, but suddenly I'm annoying and over-protective, just because you're afraid that anyone will think that you're weak or fragile because you are a woman."

"I've never given you intimate details about what I do."

"Things are different, now."

"Just go, Amir."

"If that's what you want, then alright. I'm gone."

"Goodbye."

After a few moments of tense silence, he left. She

didn't want him to go but made no move to follow him. Hanem was giving her a disapproving look, but he didn't comment. He just picked up the documents and put them back in the briefcase without a word.

"If you have something to say, say it," she said.

"I don't want you to die alone," he said.

"Everyone dies alone."

He dropped the briefcase onto the chair and crossed his arms. "You protect us, and we protect you. That is the only way this works, and if you break that bond things will fall apart before you can blink twice. You really will have no one to blame but yourself then."

"I already blame myself."

"Yes, but it isn't true yet."

He left the room before she could answer.

ELEVEN

Only one day passed before she heard from Wilson again. Instead of coming to see her in person he sent her an unmarked envelope. She found it in the midst of mail she had been sifting through in her study. It didn't even have a stamp on it. He had just slipped it into her mailbox.

She looked at the envelope for a few moments before tearing it open. She hadn't been expecting very much from him, and she was right. There was nothing but a small piece of paper with an address on it.

215 Jefferson Street
Gwynn, Virginia

Before she had a chance to recognize the address, her eyes caught sight of another letter—one that removed everything else from her mind. She opened it quickly, panic beginning to build inside her.

To Whom It May Concern:
I regret to inform you that I have decided to resign

from my position as Head of Security. I apologize for the short notice, but I have attached the names of two men I feel will do this job well.

Thank you for the opportunity
Amir Zaher

Without a second thought she left her study and went down many, many flights of stairs at a hurried pace. She entered an empty room and pulled open the wooden closet door. She knelt and felt around for the irregularity in the carpet. She finally found the edge and pealed it toward her, placing her hand on the latch beneath it and pulling a trap door open. Without bothering to properly close it behind her, she climbed down the steel ladder it revealed and dropped quietly onto the stone floor.

Amir stood by the king-sized bed in his apartment, packing the last of the three bags that lay on it. He didn't bother to fold anything. He just tossed clothes into it angrily, creating a crumpled mess that he wouldn't have the patience to iron later. The large television that took up space at the foot of his bed was so loud that he hadn't heard her come in.

She stood in silence, just watching him throw breakable items into a cardboard box on the floor. He opened his wallet and removed a picture of her she hadn't known he had and looked at it. A moment later, he tossed it into the box with everything else and closed it. He picked it up and turned, almost dropping it when he saw her.

They stood in silence, just looking at each other. He wasn't going make an effort this time. She snatched the box out of his hand and violently emptied the contents onto the floor. He made no move to stop her.

After everything had fallen out of it, she tossed the box to the ground. She looked up at him and waited for him to react, but he didn't. She grabbed the suitcase he had been packing and tossed it to the floor, but this also didn't faze him. He just looked at her without a word.

"Say something," she said.

He didn't answer her. She looked around the room for something else to ruin. Finally, she did something that sparked a reaction. She picked up the picture of her he had placed in the box and attempted to tear it. He tried to snatch it out of her hand before she could do any damage. She avoided his grasp and backed away from him, holding it. He stepped toward her and she backed into the television, almost knocking it over. In her moment of hesitation, he grabbed the photo.

She grabbed the side of the television threateningly and held her hand out for the photo, but he just took the television out of her hand and threw it across the room. It hit the wall and crashed to the floor. She grabbed the mirror on his dresser and threw it at him. He moved, and it hit the wall behind him and shattered.

She pushed him back as hard as she could, but it didn't affect him. He didn't even move. She tried again over and over, until he finally faltered and stumbled back a few inches. She kept shoving him until his back was against the wall. She started hitting him in various places of his body. He didn't try to stop her for a few moments, and then finally grabbed her wrists and held her arms to her sides. They stared at each other for a few seconds, and then he kissed her.

He entered the room, and his eyes were immediately drawn to her. She occupied a small stretch of stone floor in the corner of the room. Her face supported by feeble hands and her calves were upright and glued to her thin thighs. Despite the recoiled nature of her position, there was no trace of fear on her face. Tiredness and discomfort, perhaps, but she wasn't scared. She looked almost unconcerned.

A woman lay sprawled lifelessly to her left, her eyes wide open. There was a slit across her throat, but thick, wine-colored liquid had long since stopped falling from the cut. The corpse wasn't fresh, but this woman was still beautiful.

Long brown locks fell across her fair skin hiding her left eye from sight. Her green eyes were exuberantly rich and bright in color, even in death. Though she had been far from happy in her last moments of life, there were still traces of a smile in her expression. She hadn't been made to frown.

Yet, this beauty had never been of any interest to him. His eyes were reserved for the woman whom he could not manage to forget. Her intense blue eyes and defiant expression were embedded in his brain. He had spent hours, days, weeks, attempting to force the thought of her from his mind, but he couldn't. No matter how hard he tried to fight it she was all he thought about, and he seized every opportunity to be near her. The worst of it was, he knew she would never have him. He wasn't even permitted to see her alone.

At that moment, he knew that it was safe to see her, even if just for a few moments. With all watch guards gone, he was able to do anything, say anything, without fear of consequences. She was too weak to stop him herself. He didn't know what he was there to do, but he meant no harm. He had just wanted to see her.

He sank to the floor in front of her, bringing his face nearly at level with hers. Her expression didn't change, but she didn't speak or try to attack him. She just waited in silence to see what new torture was in store for her, but no such torture came. He didn't even touch her.

He simply held her gaze, willing her to let go of the hatred that had manifested inside her, if only just for him. The humanity she saw in him confused her. He was one of them. There was nothing remotely human about anyone who roamed free there. She hated him no less than the others, but something felt different.

She couldn't look away.

He let go and waited for her to react. She looked down and realized that his arms were still around her waist. She took a step away from him, but he remained pinned to the wall. They held each other's gaze in silence for a long moment, Jezebel trying to sort through the storm of emotions waging war inside her head, and Amir waiting for her to figure herself out. She struggled to come up with something to say that wouldn't break the spell.

"Don't go," she finally said.

He pulled her into his arms, and she shut her eyes. The tension in her body faded, and she felt his heart beat. He held her gently, letting her relax without reservation, guilt, or shame.

The strongest woman in the world, if only for a few mere moments, had found solace in the arms of another.

<u>TWELVE</u>

The house stood ominously in the dark, glowing in the light of a full moon that tinted the foreground before her. The unkempt grass had grown and then decomposed into an ugly brown. Between it lay a walkway that led to the front door, the cement so cracked that it was difficult to walk on. The door was as battered as it had always been. It was chipped in several areas and never secure enough to keep out unwanted guests. It was still standing, but all of the decorative flowers and patterns on it had faded and disappeared.

She removed the copper-made key from her front pocket slowly, holding it inches from the door for the first time in nearly two decades. It was as cold and unforgiving as the night, as if in some way berating her for abandoning it for so long. She attempted to place the key inside the lock, but her hands were so unsteady that the key fell to the ground as soon as she touched it.

Angry screams rang in her ears. A woman was standing behind the door inside, shouting curses at the caller. The unwelcome visitor pounded on the other side, returning the screams with an equal level of vigor. His words were less distinct than hers, but just as angry and vulgar.

Jezebel hastily picked up the key and unlocked the door. She pushed it open easily and walked in, leaving it open behind her. She surveyed the narrow foyer. The same tattered rug which she often had been falsely told was one of Persia's finest, lay crumpled on what was said to be a hardwood floor. The walls in the hall displayed decorative roses, which she had been told were painting on thin, cheap paper by an unnamed artist. Nothing in this house had ever been what she was told it was, including even the smallest details in her life.

The floor had several holes, some smaller and less obvious than others. She made her way through the hall and turned to her left, finding that the living room had become heavily desecrated by age. The leather black couch still sat in its original position, facing a broken television that had barely worked even in its prime. The couch was caked with dust and grime, and the television had fallen onto its face. The glass shattered, and small shards were all over the room.

To the left of it all, a large window that looked out onto the street took up most of the wall. A small couch sat underneath it.

The woman stormed through the room and ran to another door directly across from her on the back wall. Before she could reach it, a man rushed in, caught her arm, and dragged her to him. She attempted to push him off, but he grabbed her hair. She dug her long, sharp nails into his forearm. He cried out in pain and let go of her. She took the opportunity to slap him so hard that her palm imprinted on his cheek. Before she took more than two steps—

"This is a pleasant surprise."

Jezebel looked up, and in the doorway of the kitchen stood none other than Detective Asher Wilson. Her jaw tightened at the sight of the obnoxious, condescending smirk on his face.

"Get out," she said.

"You're always trying to kick me out. It's hurtful, you know."

"You're trespassing, Shepherd."

His smile faded. "Wilson."

"You are not welcome here."

"What are you going to do? Call the police?"

"Yes. I'm just not sure which detective to complain about."

"Stay out of my personal business."

"After you."

"I didn't come to argue with you. You aren't going to leave me out of this investigation."

"I told you not to give me orders."

"I already searched every inch of this house. Are there hiding places, or maybe safes?"

"If you're going to be here, shut up and stay out of the way."

"Fine. I'll just watch."

She ignored him and returned to the hallway and climb the rickety, unsafe, stairs. Each step groaned loudly and shook under her. Only half of the banister had remained intact. A large part of it had given up and fallen to its death in pieces.

There were only two rooms on the second floor, both of them very small. Four bare walls boxed in nothing more than a bed. It was just big enough to fit two people and a small child.

The door was closed, but she heard voices inside.

She had finally grown just tall enough to reach the doorknob, and she clumsily turned it. It opened only a few inches, and she stuck her head through the opening. The man had backed the woman up to the wall, but she was not protesting here. She was breathing heavily, and for some reason she wasn't fully dressed. Suddenly, a little boy yanked her away from the door and shut it quickly.

"Go to bed," he said.

"Are you alright?"

She blinked several times, and then exited the room and closed the door.

"There is nothing to see here," she said.

"Whose room was this?"

She went to the stairs and ignored him.

"Jezebel?"

"None of your business."

"You grew up here, right?"

"Stop asking me questions."

"I'm helping."

"If you want to help, go home."

"I'm sorry if I forced an unwanted memory on you."

"You can't force me into anything."

"If returning to this house is painful for you, just quit. I've been digging through it for hours and haven't found anything."

"No one is better suited to search this house than I am. If you're going to be here, be quiet. You should consider yourself lucky that I'm even allowing you to intrude on my personal property. Don't push me."

She quickly descended the stairs and sat on the black couch without bothering to dust it off first. She tried to force herself to think clearly and push the unwanted emotions aside, but it was difficult. This house still filled her with anxiety, even so many years later.

She sat at the window, attempting to read a book and tune out the mayhem taking place around her. Her eyes were trained on the page as two people who could not seem to keep it together or successfully part ways tore each other to shreds. It was often so violent that blood was shed.

The story she was reading was that of an adventure she longed to take. Her hero was a heartless murderer. Protagonists were ultimately all the same. It was the villain who made the story special.

The crashing sound of glass broke through her dreams as a crystal vase flew through the air. It missed her nose by inches, colliding with the window she rested on. A gaping hole was left in the place of the impact, and the vase broke in half and rolled into the street. The violent noise that she had managed to tune out suddenly returned. The woman was bleeding in various places and screaming like a banshee. The man who had created the injuries covered her mouth, and she bit his palm and kicked him in an area that no male could stand pain. He released her and cried out, doubling over and falling to his knees.

The moment he let go of her, the woman ran into another room and returned with a knife. She held it away from her body, wielding it toward the weakened man on the floor, tears falling in rivers along her face. She looked frozen in place. She didn't attempt to use it at all.

The man recovered and stood. He made no move to assault her. He just waited for the woman to attempt an attack, but she didn't. Instead, her arms fell limply to her sides, and she slowly walked out of the room and disappeared up the stairs. The man watched her go, and then went to the front door. He opened it slightly, and then looked back at the mess he was leaving behind.

The girl watching them had stayed silent and remained in her seat for the duration of the fight. It was a common occurrence in this house. Nothing they did surprised her anymore. He turned to the child slowly and a small, bitter smile formed on his face.

"When you miss me, you will find me in the walls."

It was the final moment she was to see him for a very long time.

Jezebel straightened, and it dawned on her exactly why she had been brought back to this house. She hadn't been brought back here to relive any memories. Nothing but demons and sadness had ever lived here.

She stood and looked around.

"What are you looking for?" Wilson asked.

"Something heavy."

She went up the stairs and entered the room she had avoided before. Two small beds were adjacent to walls opposite each other. The white paint was relatively undamaged, with just a few chips having fallen here and there. The room was much cleaner than any other area in the house. It was almost as if someone had been making sure it remained intact.

She found a metal bat covered in dust at the foot of one of the beds. She picked it up just as Wilson walked into the room. He had found a rusted axe she had never seen before. She didn't acknowledge him, but he held her arm before she started her attack on the wall.

"Take the axe and give me the bat," he said.

"Just get the hell out of my house, Wilson."

"Don't be emotional. Take the axe. You won't be able to do anything with that bat, but I can."

"I don't need your help."

"Maybe not, but you do need something stronger

than just a useless piece of metal."

She grudgingly handed him the bat and took the axe. She turned to the wall by her bed and gathered every ounce of physical strength she had. She swung the sharp blade back and then directly into the wall. It broke through immediately. Wilson started making similar attacks on the opposite end of the same wall.

Large pieces of white paint exploded from it, shooting across the room and onto their clothes and faces. They broke through the thin wood easily, and pieces of it fell away. Instead of finding themselves seeing the next room, they found an empty space between the wall they had broken and the wall of the bathroom. In the middle of the space sat a small safe.

Wilson picked it up and put it on the bed. Neither of them made a move to open it. They stood together, staring at it, unsure of how to proceed. As expected, Wilson was the first to break the silence.

"Do you know the code?" he asked.

"No."

"Trial and error."

"I'm not opening this in front of you."

"You can't carry it on your own and I'm not helping you or leaving."

"I can carry it."

"Go ahead. I won't stop you."

She bent and picked it up just a few inches before dropping it again. The thing weighed no less than sixty pounds. Wilson was fairly built; it wouldn't be difficult for him to move it. She stepped aside.

"Your pride is going to get you killed," he said.

"Your nosiness is going to get you killed."

"Just open it."

Jezebel took a seat on the floor in front of it and entered the only numerical value that she could remember. Surprisingly, the lock immediately popped open, and she pulled the little iron door.

A mess of papers lay inside. She set them all on the bed, and then picked one of them up. It was the deed to the house, and it was in her name. She sifted through more of the documents and found that many other valuable things had been left for her: checks for hundreds of thousands of dollars, codes to several bank accounts, and properties that had been bought in her name. None of this excited her, until she came upon something she hadn't expected to find. It was a letter from her father.

My Darling Jezebel,

If this letter has come into your possession, then I have likely joined your mother in death.

I know that you will never forgive me for the mistakes I have made. I am not so foolish to believe that there is redemption for what I have done, but you have my regrets and apologies, just the same. Not a night passes that I don't think of you and your mother. She and I fought constantly, but please believe me when I say that there is no one on this earth that I have loved more than her, aside from you.

I do not expect you to believe that.

I know that the wealth I left for you here is not what you ever needed from me, but this is all that is left for me to pass on to you. I have many mementoes from your childhood, but I know that leaving them here would be pointless. You would have thrown it all out.

There are other things in this safe that I left for you, but they are not gifts. I made many enemies in my life, and I suspect that you only returned to this house to search for answers that may help you defeat your own. I don't know how you made them or why, but your decision to come here can only mean that you are fighting to avoid the end that I have met.

Everything in this safe has been put there for a reason. Do not disregard anything I'm giving you. I wouldn't leave them here to waste your time. I know that you have no reason to trust me, but I am still your father. I would never purposely let you get hurt, Jezebel.

Begin with the list of addresses. I would rather you not visit them, as they may be covered in traps. Send someone to inspect them in your place. You may not be as selfish as I am, but just this one time, save your own skin before you worry for the lives of the people around you.

I don't expect you to forgive me, but I cannot end this last exchange between us with anything other than my sincerest love and affection.

You are my only daughter.
I love you.
-Dad

She crumpled the letter and tossed it back into the safe.

"I am sorry for your loss, Jezebel."

"Don't be. It wasn't a loss."

"You aren't as selfish as I thought you were."

She looked at him. "No. I'm worse."

"You're not alone there."

"Said the vessel of justice?"

"You already know that my purpose in this investigation has nothing to do with enforcing the law. There's no need to be so condescending."

She returned her attention to the papers in front of her. "I'm naturally condescending."

"What was it like, growing up here?"

"You have no right to ask me anything."

"Your childhood must have been difficult."

"Stop making assumptions about me!"

"I had a difficult childhood, too."

"I don't care."

"My mother was gone my entire life."

She looked at him. "Why are you telling me this?"

"Because even though I know you're a criminal in one way or another, I don't want to hurt you anymore."

"I'm *not* a charity case. My childhood was fine."

"I was born to a very rich family."

"Congratulations."

"But my father was abusive, too."

"My father was not abusive."

"We aren't so different."

"We couldn't be more different."

He was silent for a few seconds and then said, "You have my word that I will do my best to keep you out of this investigation, Jezebel."

She turned to him. "Why?"

He ran his hand through his hair, his eyes a darker, more somber, blue than she had noticed in him before.

"Because we are more alike than I thought we were."

"Just because baby Wilson didn't like his daddy doesn't mean we are in any way similar."

"In time, you will see things my way."

"I don't intend on spending any time with you."

"Intentions don't matter."

"You don't know what you're dealing with."

"I know, but I will."

Without another word, they both returned their attention to the papers. She found the list of addresses he had mentioned in the letter. There were only three, none of them were in Virginia. She put the list in her back pocket and closed the safe door, leaving the inheritance inside.

"Not going to take any of it?" Wilson asked.

"No."

THIRTEEN

Three days later Jezebel sat alone in an Italian restaurant, *"Quintessence."* She had ordered a cup of coffee but it remained untouched. She took the menu from the table and looked down at it. She had worn her pin-straight hair down to use it to hide her face from the table to her far right. It wasn't time for them to notice her presence yet. She wanted to be the very last thing the people sitting there saw before they were dragged out against their will.

There were two tables between her and the couple who were the center of her attention. The man was talking more than the woman who was with him, not giving her a chance to get a word in. He was incapable of holding his tongue for long periods of time, and often said things that would annoy the people around him on purpose. Because he was a coward he constantly apologized for the offensive things he said, whether he had truly meant them or not.

Amir slammed himself down into the seat across from her. He looked extremely angry, but she didn't care. She smiled mockingly and took a sip of the coffee in front of her.

"Yes, Amir?"

"I thought you were going to stop."

"What are you talking about?"

"Why are you doing this?"

"I don't know what you're so angry about."

"The hell you don't."

"I'm not leaving you out."

"You sent Adel! You sent my twin brother and three other people with that idiotic detective and left me in the dark!"

"Calm down."

"How can you do this again? I thought—"

"Lower your voice."

He sat back in his chair and waited.

"I didn't send you because it's very likely that there are traps set up in those places, and you're never careful. There was no reason for you to go with them and put yourself in danger."

His eyes narrowed. "You're treating me like I am a weak little girl who can't defend herself."

"Feels awful, doesn't it?

"So this is just revenge."

"No, but I can't say it doesn't feel good to watch you suffer through your frustration."

"You're trying to get me back for being overbearing."

"So you admit that you've been taking your obsessive need to protect me too far then?"

"It's warranted! You have many enemies and things are more dangerous than ever right now!"

"I can take care of myself."

"You said you wouldn't do this to me anymore."

"I didn't do it to annoy you."

"Why did you leave me out? Why did you send that detective? He's trying to throw us all in jail!"

"I don't want you to deliberately put yourself in danger. I don't care if that upsets you."

"I am not a child."

"Neither am I."

"It's not the same. You hired me to do this."

"You claim that you want to protect me. Well, I'm here, not there. If you're willing to leave me unarmed and alone then I will gladly hand over every address your dying little heart desires."

"You're manipulating me."

"And it's working."

He fought with himself for several seconds and then said, "Fine. I'll stay here with you."

She sat back in her chair and said, "You go on and enjoy your day."

He gave her a patronizing smile and leaned forward. "Say what you want, but the only reason you didn't send me was that you were worried about my safety. You were afraid I'd get hurt and leave you alone, and you are too in love with me to let that happen."

Her amusement died. "Not true."

"Then why?"

"I am not afraid to be alone. I've been alone before, and I didn't need you to be there to protect me."

"Answer my question."

"No. I don't care what you think."

"You love me."

He immediately stood and walked out of the restaurant. She returned her gaze to the table she had come to watch and waited patiently. The man emptied the entire bottle of wine into their glasses, and he and the woman he was with started whispering to each other. Jezebel had been under the impression that he didn't drink due to some kind of illness, but she wasn't surprised. The man rarely told the truth.

Jules sat down in front of her, raising her eyebrows.

"What?" she asked.

"Is he going to get arrested here?"

"Yes."

"Don't."

"Do not tell me what to do."

"Please."

"This was your idea!"

"I reacted badly because I thought he betrayed me, but I don't think he did. He didn't do anything to deserve this."

"Do you really believe that Bugsy Marcel didn't kill Athena Elias, or are you just protecting him?"

"I think someone set him up."

"Did he or did he not murder her?"

"He did, but not to hurt you!"

"Who set him up?"

"It doesn't matter."

"It does matter. Give me a reason why I shouldn't let them throw him in jail for the rest of his miserable life."

"He didn't hurt you, Jezebel."

"Yes, he did."

"He didn't come anywhere near you or your business. He has always just been jealous that a woman could be more successful than he has ever been. He made mistakes, but he's human."

"If I don't do this my reputation will be ruined."

"It won't! You're too sensitive because you think everyone looks down on you for being a woman!"

"Watch what you say to me."

"I'm not trying to offend you, but he is my partner."

"Why did you work with him, Jules? He's neither talented nor tolerable. What's kept you loyal to him for so long?"

"He is my partner, no matter what."

"Love really is blind, isn't it?"

"What?"

Not two seconds later, eight men clad in police uniforms stormed into the restaurant. The man at the head of the group surveyed the room, and then caught sight of the couple she had been watching. He stormed over to the table and looked down at the man.

Jules immediately dove under the table to keep himself out of direct line of vision. The linen was dragged to the side, and her mug fell over and hit him in the head. The hot coffee spilled onto his shoulder, but he didn't react.

"Bugsy Marcel, you are under arrest for the murder of Athena Elias," the officer said.

"NO!" the woman yelled.

"WHAT THE HELL ARE YOU TALKING ABOUT?" Marcel yelled and knocked over his wine glass.

Two officers pulled him to his feet and put his wrists in handcuffs behind his back, and one of them said, "You have the right to remain silent. Anything you say can and will be used against you in a court of law. You have the right to an attorney. If you cannot afford an attorney, one will be appointed to you by the state."

Marcel turned and ran, but before he could move more than a few feet they caught him. He relaxed his body, trying to make it more difficult for them to pull him out of the restaurant, but it didn't work. There were too many of them, and a further resist of arrest would only add to his charges. The woman with him, his sister, burst into a melodramatic hysteria as she watched the scene unfold before her. She pushed the table over onto its side, screaming out something indiscernible in the process. The people at the tables next to them jumped up and backed away quickly.

Marcel looked around the room frantically and caught sight of her just as they dragged him out. She winked and gave him a small wave. Extreme hostility covered his face, but before he could so much as say one word he was carted off. He tripped over his own feet in the process, almost knocking down a few of the officers around him. He relaxed his body again, and the police officers resorted to dragging him out of the door. They left his sister behind to work herself into a panic attack, which no one around her seemed to care about. A few moments later, she also stood and left. Their waiter was holding their bill, unsure what to do with it. He looked too afraid to follow either one of them.

Jezebel motioned for the waiter to come over to her, and she said, "Give me their bill."

The waiter raised his eyebrows. "Are you sure?"

"Yes."

"Okay." He handed her their bill over and quickly walked away.

Jezebel sat back and crossed her arms, reveling in the victory. Seeing Bugsy Marcel publicly humiliated was infinitely more satisfying than watching him suffer through physical torture. Jules, however, didn't share that feeling at all. He looked like he was in actual pain.

"Please, don't leave him in jail," he said.

"It's too late. You should have come to me earlier. I gave Wilson more than enough evidence to indict him."

"Would you have let him go if I had?"

"What answer would torment you less?"

"Tell me that you wouldn't have let him go regardless of whether I helped you or not."

"I wouldn't have let him go, regardless of whether you help me or not."

He stood up. "Thank you."

"What's the point in torturing yourself with what may have been? Leave the past where it belongs."

"I could ask you the same thing."

"Your partner made his bed. Let him rot in it."

"Give him another chance."

"I have no reason to."

Hanem appeared in front of her. "They're back."

"This quickly?"

He looked at Jules. "Why are you here?"

"It was worth a try."

"I told you not to come to her with this!"

"I had to try, Hanem!"

"Marcel isn't worth it, Jules!"

"That isn't up to you to decide!"

"You met behind my back?" Jezebel asked.

"He came to the office when you were out last night. I didn't have time to reach you, and it wasn't that important."

"Were you going to tell me?"

"We need to go, Jezebel. Yell at me later."

"Come on."

She stood to leave, but Jules held her. "Jezebel, you can help anyone escape from anywhere. Just get him out, even if he is indicted. You can do it. You can do almost anything."

"He is safer in prison."

"I can protect him out here."

"You will find another partner, Jules."

"I don't want another partner, Jezebel."

She looked at him silently for a moment and then said, "Find someone else to fall in love with. You can do so much better."

She and Hanem walked out of the restaurant, leaving Jules at the table. She found a black car waiting outside for her. They got into the backseat of the car quickly, and the driver immediately took off. She didn't recognize the man behind the wheel, which would not be unusual under any other circumstances.

She leaned over to Hanem and whispered, "Who is that in the driver's seat? I don't recognize him."

"I know him. I wouldn't trust a stranger to drive you anywhere, especially not now."

"Alright."

"Was Jules begging you to get Marcel out of prison?"

"Yes. When did he come to you?"

"Yesterday, and I said no."

"I don't understand his attitude."

"You would if it was Amir."

The drive back to her office was maddeningly slow. It was just after six, and the city's traffic was at the height of its congestion. She looked out of her window, watching the people in other vehicles and on foot, living their lives around her. Drivers in New York City were naturally angry. She had found in the past that even the kindest of them became different people behind the wheel. Their driving became erratic, vocabulary vulgar, and blood pressure shot far higher than average. It was the New York Effect, and no one was immune.

After about an hour, the driver pulled into the practice's parking lot. Jezebel stepped out and walked in through the front door. She wasn't worried that Wilson would be poking around inside, sticking his nose where it didn't belong. Plenty of people would prevent that.

Amir, Adel, Wilson and two other men were standing uncomfortably inside her office. She sat behind the desk and folded her hands. Amir and Wilson both looked annoyed, but she didn't ask.

"What did you find?" she asked.

"The first two addresses were apartments, and they were completely empty," Wilson said. "There wasn't even furniture. They were just empty rooms inside rundown buildings. It looked like no one had been there in a long time."

"And the third?"

Wilson placed a stack of papers on the desk. "This

was all we found, but they aren't interesting. They're just scraps of empty paper, and promotional mail and magazines."

Jezebel sifted through the papers carefully, and just as she was about to put them down and accept that she had reached a dead end, something caught her eye. It was a business card for *Quintessence*, and there was a number and a name on the back: Michael Saint.

"Have you ever heard of a man named Michael Saint?" she asked Hanem and handed him the card.

He looked it over. "Yes. He runs the restaurant. This must be his personal phone number. The restaurant is in a different area code."

"Who chose the restaurant I was just in?"

"Jules said it was Marcel's favorite restaurant. That is why he sent him there for us today."

"That doesn't make sense. It's common knowledge that Bugsy has always notoriously been allergic to Italian food."

"Ironic," Amir said.

"As if you know what that word means," Wilson said.

"Stop," Hanem snapped before Amir could respond, and then looked back at her. "Bugsy was never honest about anything a day in his life, Jezebel. It doesn't surprise me that he lied."

"Yes, but he has allergic reactions to any kind of pasta, and *Quintessence* is famous for those dishes," Amir said. "I've seen him get sick from it myself more than once."

"And Bugsy wouldn't lie to Jules, and Jules has no reason to lie to us," Hanem said.

"Exactly," Jezebel said.

"What are you getting at?" Amir asked.

She ignored the question; instead, "Who owns the restaurant?"

"I don't know, but I can find out."

"Make an appointment for me to meet him."

"Why?"

"Just do it. In the meantime, I want you to find every bit of information you can about that restaurant."

"Alright."

"What are you thinking, Jezebel?" Wilson asked.

"You're not stupid. Don't pretend to be."

"That was the nicest thing you have ever said to me."

"Don't get used to it," Amir snapped.

"You stay out of it," Wilson said.

"Make me."

"What are *you* going to—"

"Get out," Jezebel snapped. "Both of you, get the hell out of my office right now."

FOURTEEN

Jezebel adjusted the thick, dark glasses and moved some loose strands of the blonde wig she wore to fall across her face. Then, she stepped into the restaurant. She extended the stick she was holding and moved it around on the floor in front of her. Her eyes darted around the room quickly, taking in how many people would get caught in the crosshairs if Amir and Wilson were reckless. Judging only by their inability to have a civil conversation, this was extremely likely.

Along with Hanem, they were sitting in a corner, as far away from the front as possible. Wilson and Amir were looking anywhere but at each other, and Hanem was pretending to look over the menu. He always did what was asked of him, but it would be impossible to control them if they provoked each other enough to start a physical fight.

About twenty patrons sat at tables all around. Most of them were elderly people who did not have jobs to worry about on a weekday's afternoon, and quite a few of them were dining alone. A cluster of men in business suits were sitting at a table in the back. They were clearly attending a work-related lunch and weren't paying attention to anything around them. A young couple sat by the window that looked out on the street, sharing their food and laughing. The man was wearing a wedding ring, but she was not. He was having an affair in broad daylight, like an idiot.

Aside from these few people, the restaurant was dead.

"Can I help you to your table, madam?" a small man of about thirty asked her.

"I'm here to see Michael Saint," Jezebel said. "We had an appointment to meet at half past noon. I've been waiting for several minutes now."

"I apologize. I didn't see you. Let me show you to his office."

"Thank you."

Jezebel held his forearm and let him lead her to an office in the back of the restaurant. He opened the door, helped her find the chair, and then left. She looked around the room, taking in how poor the taste of the man who had decorated this office was.

It was simply a small, plain office. There was a window so small that something no bigger than a cat could fit through it, and there was very little ventilation. The walls were a simple white color, and a standard gray carpet covered the floor. The metal desk in front of her was the only piece of furniture in the room, aside from the chair behind it and the chair she sat in. Perhaps he hadn't thought about aesthetics at all, or maybe he had another place he managed his business. Either way, the room was no sight for sore eyes.

A few minutes later a thin, blonde man walked in. He was remarkably tall, and his complexion was a warm tan color that was clearly an attempt to look younger than he was. It clashed with his green eyes, and only brought attention to the wrinkles on his face. He had a tattoo of a cobra on his left forearm.

He shut the door tightly and sat in the chair behind his desk. He gave her a plastic smile and leaned back in the chair, crossing his arms. He clearly had no desire to speak to her at all.

"How can I help you, Miss Rose?" he asked.

"I had an unpleasant experience here the other night," Jezebel said. "And I don't take kindly to mistreatment merely because I can't see the expressions people wear when they serve me."

"What happened?"

"One of your waiters spoke to me condescendingly when I asked him to read me the specials. I'm not going to stand for discrimination against people with disabilities. Are you aware that I could sue you?"

"That's unacceptable. Did you catch his name?"

"He didn't introduce himself, and if I can't read the menu, do you think I'd have been able to read his nametag?"

He cleared his throat. "I apologize. How can I help?"

"Do I look familiar to you, Mr. Saint?"

"No, but those glasses cover up nearly half of your lovely face."

"Don't flatter me."

"It was meant as a joke."

"I didn't come here to socialize."

"On the phone, you told me that your name is Kristine."

"My father is Joseph Rose."

His eyes widened, and he sat up in the chair. "*The* Joseph Rose?"

"One of the most powerful people in this city, yes. Do you know what Joseph Rose does when his only daughter is unhappy?"

"I assure you, madam, this mistake will be taken

care of! You didn't hear anyone call his name?"

"No."

"Would you like me to bring them all to you?"

"No. I was disrespected and mistreated here. I would like something to make up for that."

"What can I offer?"

"I want a stake in the restaurant."

"Really?"

"Yes. The food here is exceptional, and the restaurant is very famous."

"I-well—"

"Why are you hesitating?"

"It's just surprising."

"You don't look excited."

"I can hear it in your voice."

"Well—"

He was interrupted by a crashing sound outside of the door. They heard yelling and things breaking. It sounded as though an extremely violent fight was taking place in the dining room. She knew exactly who was causing it, but it had come too soon. They had been instructed to wait twenty minutes before doing anything at all.

He stood quickly. "Please excuse me. I'll be right back."

He left and closed the door behind him.

"Can't follow simple directions," she said to herself, and then went around the desk and sat in his chair. She began opening the drawers and rummaging through the items inside but nothing was important, and it didn't seem as if he used it very often. The three drawers on her right held nothing but a stapler, glue, a picture of a golden retriever, and scissors. The two on the right were empty. Atop the desk were blank sheets of paper and a cup full of pens. Colorful paper clips were scattered everywhere. Nothing looked as though it had been touched in a long time.

She sat back and looked around the room for another possible hiding spot. Concealed in a corner by the window was a two-drawer file cabinet. She rushed over to it and opened the first one, but it was empty. The second one was locked. She tried to force it open, but it didn't budge. She turned and went back to the desk in search of keys. She went through the desk again, but they weren't there.

The lights suddenly went out, and the light being shed into the room was too weak to be helpful. She took off the glasses to reduce the visual impairment, but it was still difficult to see everything clearly. The shouting outside of the door intensified, and she almost felt the grains of sand fall through an hour glass that represented just how quickly her time was running out.

Her eyes darted around the small office, and she saw a jacket hanging on the back of the door. She pulled it off the hanger and went through the pockets. Sure enough, there was a ring of keys in the left pocket. She quickly went back to the file cabinet. There were at least fifty keys on the ring, and the shouting outside of the door was beginning to die down.

Instead of trying to go in order, she picked a random key and jammed it into the lock. It actually went in, but it refused to turn. It also refused to come out. She fell to her knees and grappled with it. She pulled so hard that her fingers hurt, but nothing happened. She gave it one final tug, and the entire cabinet came out, its contents spilling out onto the floor.

An entire file full of papers lay in a heap before her. Without sparing a moment to think, she gathered them all and stuffed them into her purse. She pushed the cabinet back into place and removed the trapped key from the ring. Then, she stuck the ring back into his jacket pocket and retook her seat.

Not thirty seconds later, Saint walked back into the office looking disheveled and extremely angry. His face had turned an uninviting shade of puce and his white shirt was torn at his left side.

"What the hell is going on?" she asked.

He took a deep breath. "I apologize, but can this meeting be rescheduled for another time?"

"Yes. It was good to meet you. I hope everything is okay."

"I trust that this won't become a problem with your father?"

She laughed lightly. "You should never trust a woman you don't know, Mr. Saint. Good day."

She walked out of his office and shut the door behind her. She looked around at the aftermath. No patrons were left. Tables were overturned, and shattered glass and food covered the floor. Most of the employees had gotten caught in the crosshairs. Three of them were hiding behind an overturned table, and four more were just standing in the middle of the room, trying to figure out where to proceed from here. The mess would take hours to clean thoroughly. She pitied the people who would be saddled with the responsibility.

She left the building and was pulled into a limousine with blacked out windows. When she had settled into a seat in the back she took off the glasses and the wig. She was alone with the driver, whom she recognized as Adel when her eyes had adjusted to the daylight. He gave her a wide smile—an odd thing that wasn't customary of him—and drove away from the restaurant.

"Why are you driving me, Adel?"

"Hanem asked me to."

"And why a limousine?"

"I don't ask questions, Jezebel."

"Alright."

Just a few minutes later he pulled over, and none other than Wilson, Amir, and Hanem joined her in the car. Two of the three were sporting injuries: Wilson's nose was broken, and Amir had a cut that stretched from the edge of his left eyebrow to the corner of his mouth. There was blood all over their clothes. Neither seemed to have noticed or cared.

"Why are you injured?" she demanded.

"You asked for a diversion, didn't you?" Wilson snapped.

"Watch your tone," Amir said.

"Or what?" Wilson asked.

"You don't actually think that you have a chance to beat me in a fight, Shepherd?"

"Don't call me that."

"Stop!" Jezebel said. "Are you children? Do I have to send you to your rooms until you've decided it's time for you to start acting like adults?"

"He started it," they both said.

"Excuse me?" Wilson asked. "You are the one who was exhibiting typical jealous escort behavior!"

"What the hell do you mean by '*escort*,' you disgusting—"

"Not another WORD!" Jezebel yelled.

Both immediately fell silent.

"Hanem, what happened?" she asked.

Hanem, who had been giving the other two disapproving glares, said, "They got into a fight five minutes before their cue and caused a scene that was much more violent than necessary. People ran out screaming and two waitresses fell over tables and onto broken glass. It was an absolute disaster."

"Don't be dramatic, Hanem," Amir said.

"Dramatic? I had to cut off the electricity to keep them from calling the police and throwing you both in jail."

"I am the police," Wilson said.

"And if you keep up this behavior you won't be for much longer."

"He belongs in jail," Wilson said.

"You belong on the street," Amir said.

"Where you were born, I'm sure."

"Listen to me, both of you," Jezebel said. "You will move past this pointless feud of yours, and you will learn to tolerate each other. Otherwise, you can both mosey on back into your basic respective jobs and stay out of this completely."

Neither responded. Hanem handed both of them cloth napkins. Amir grudgingly thanked him, but Wilson did not. They cleaned their faces and then threw the napkins out of the window.

Jezebel removed the papers from her bag and handed half of them to Hanem, ignoring the outstretched hands of the other two. She started reading, and Amir attempted to take a few from her, but she slapped his hand away. He crossed his arms and waited silently.

She combed through the stack carefully, but every single page was blank. It began to seem like a fruitless endeavor until she found something. In the middle of the stack of empty white lay a paper that she was sure would cause an uproar as soon as Saint realized it was missing.

Hanem noticed her staring and asked, "You found something?"

She handed it to him. "Look."

"The deed," he said.

"To the restaurant?" Wilson asked.

"No, the library," Amir said. "Of course the restaurant."

"It could be fake," Hanem said.

"Why would he hide a fake deed?" Jezebel asked.

"Where did you find it?"

"In a locked cabinet."

"Look at the bottom. It's notarized."

"Could be counterfeit," Amir said.

"I can always tell the difference," Hanem said. "This is a real legal document, but from what I know about this place, it can't be possible."

"What did you find out?" she asked.

"The building itself was built in 1957 and used as a brothel," he said. "It was shut down, and then reopened in 1975 by one Michael Saint, who bought the building and turned it into a restaurant."

"That doesn't seem impossible."

"Yes, but the original owner was Hadley Scott, and he supposedly died in prison in 1973. The building was possessed by the state and sold to Michael Saint two years after his death."

"And you are absolutely sure that Hadley Scott died before Saint bought the building?"

"Yes."

She showed him the document again. "Then how is it possible that he signed this deed himself?"

"That's what's confusing me. Scott died two years before Michael Saint even left California for New York."

"The date noted here is December 31, 1975, and it says that Hadley Scott was the seller."

"Maybe the notary was in their pocket."

"But whose pocket?"

"I don't know."

"And you found no information on Hadley Scott himself? Medical history, background, other assets?"

"Nothing of significance. There were no listed family members or addresses. I couldn't even find his arrest records or why he ended up in jail. I just know that he had been in there for three years before he died."

Jezebel was silent for a long moment and then asked, "Do you know where Scott is buried?"

"You aren't considering digging up a grave, Jezebel?"

"I asked you a question."

"New Jersey."

"Southern?"

"Central."

"You and I—"

"You are not going to leave me here," Amir said. "I'm not going to be left in the dark again."

Jezebel turned her cold eyes on him. "Do not *ever* cut me off when I'm speaking."

"You won't go without me. No matter what you say. I'm head of your security. I go where you go."

"And you can't stop me from coming either," Wilson said. "I do not work for you, Jezebel White."

Adel pulled the car to a stop, and she opened the door. "Go home. I have nothing to say to either of you. Your behavior today proved that you are both more a liability than you are an assistance. I don't have time to get into this with either of you, and Hanem is not a babysitter. He has actual responsibilities, and both of you can go to hell for all I care."

Before anyone could respond, she vacated her seat and slammed the car door behind her, leaving them to tear each other to pieces.

<u>FIFTEEN</u>

The wind that plagued the dark stretch of land lamented in soft wails in the night, adding to the unnerving atmosphere and casting an eerie spell. It wasn't forceful or angry. It was an uncomfortable addition to an empty night, but still only harmless sound.

The cold that coated the cemetery was biting, creating a tangible thin layer of ice upon all that it touched. It gently drained circulation from all life that dared come here, and no sane creature did. No amount of clothing could combat it. It chilled every bone and ran shivers down every spine.

The sky was cruelly unleashing a rainfall that rivaled the torrential showers of Cropp River. The water so heavy that grass was overcome with thick, wet sludge. The clouds that loomed above were dark and uninviting. They casted an ugly asylum over the moon, blocking its light.

The rain that hailed from above them created a strained silence in the air. Even with so many people present, it remained undeterred, deafening, crushing, and—for the moment—still. No sound could drown it out as it dominated the night, making all else that existed there invisible and obsolete. The party that had brought themselves into its hands kept the quiet in a brief halted daze, taking no action but trying to take in their surroundings. It was like a clichéd scene from a generic horror film.

They stood on a patch of unhealthy muddy grass, encircled by the headstones that marked the dead around them. The graves were dug in rings, and they were standing in the center with backs to each other. Their eyes not couldn't see far enough to calculate the distance they would likely have to go or how far away from one another they would end up being.

Lightning suddenly cracked through the gloom above them. Without sparing looks at each other, the group separated and headed in different directions. It was extremely difficult to read every stone, and the rain was no help at all. The oversized flashlights were helpful only when they were pushed an inch or two away from the inscriptions.

She shined the light as close to the gravestone as possible and read the name. Unsurprisingly, the first grave was not the one they were searching for. The stone they were attempting to find was much farther from the center of the graveyard. She looked around to see where everyone else had gone and found that Hanem was working on the innermost circle. She ventured six rings out.

Instead of moving in full circles, she decided to search half of each ring. The others would be checking the other side. She had to clear mud off of every stone she reached in order to see the words, but this was by far the easiest part of her task. Many of the stones themselves were cracked and faded. She squinted to read the writing and traced them with her fingers, hoping to put together the words by recognizing the letters. This was a successful method on quite a few, but none of them were what she was looking for.

Just as she bent to check another grave toward the end of the sixth circle, she lost her footing and fell flat on her stomach, sliding a few feet forward and covering herself in thick, rancid mud. The sweater she wore had gone from gray to an ugly brown and was soaked through. She pushed the disgust out of her mind and tried to stand.

She found, however, that it was far easier to see and move when in closer proximity to the ground. She got up onto her hands and knees, and then began to crawl. Dragging the shovel was no easy task, but she managed to reach behind her every few minutes to pull it along. She was moving slowly, but she was in less danger in this position than when she attempted to walk on two feet and bend over. She had never been graceful, and another fall could break her neck or cause a concussion.

Much to her dismay, at the beginning of the seventh ring, she dropped the flashlight. Her heart dropped into her stomach as she frantically dug through the dirt, her nails suffering from the effort. She pulled it out of the mud and cleaned it off with her sweater. She flipped the switch to turn it off and then back on, but nothing happened. After a minute of fiddling with it, she gave up. She threw it back in the dirt and resorted to waiting for lightning to crack in order to catch a glimpse of the words. Each grave took several minutes longer now.

Her back was beginning to ache, and her hair and body had reached a level of filth she was unfamiliar with. She took another fall into the dirt, and this time her face was not saved from being soiled. Water invaded her nostrils and mouth, causing her to gag and her stomach to turn. As she struggled to regulate her breathing, she wondered how the others were fairing.

Amir was likely struggling to remain steady the most. He was too big for this to be easy for him. Hanem's eyes were useless without his glasses, and a single fall could easily break them. She knew too little about Wilson to judge whether he would struggle here or not.

The seventh ring proved to be a complete disaster. Instead of simple gravestones, each plot was headed up by a statue of some sort. They were of different sizes, and she was forced to get up and crouch back down periodically, increasing the pain in her back. What was worse, all of them were white, making the level of difficulty of reading by lightning strike increase tenfold.

A number of them were upright creations that portrayed animals known to be symbols of strength and pride. Others were awkward busts of the bodies she assumed were buried beneath them. Many of them were also more disturbing than they were noble. Three of them were chiseled into the shape of deformed centaurs. Each had only one eye that was too large in proportion to the rest of its head, and the mouth spread from the area where there should have been a nose to the very edge of its chin. At a closer glance, she saw that the three graves held men with the same last name. They were most likely brothers, and they had died on the same night; a fetish for the gruesome clearly ran in the family.

At the middle of the eighth ring, something wonderful happened. She found it. Here was the grave of Hadley Scott, and after a few minutes of trying to read it completely, she saw the date. Hadley Scott had indeed died on the 31st of December in 1973, and any leads she may have had now lay here in this grave with him. She sat back on her heals and read the inscription:

'Liar, liar, the dead's on fire.'

She read it twice, struggling to make sense of it, and then gave up. She reached into her back pocket and pointed a flare gun above her head. She pulled the trigger, and red light shot into the sky. She put it down and sat cross-legged on the ground, abandoning all previous attempts to stay clean and accepting the grime as a newfound part of her body.

After a few minutes' rest, she took a deep breath and stood. She dug her shovel into the ground, but after each pile of dirt she threw out, more slid down to replace it. What little upper body strength she had was waning, and she began to regret having been the one to find it.

Five minutes of failed digging later, two familiar figures appeared by her side. Both gently stopped her and took on the challenge she had been failing at. She dropped her shovel and stepped back to watch. Wilson's shovel broke in half, and she handed him her own. He tossed his aside violently, and it hit one of the centaurs, chipping a piece of it off.

Amir and Wilson shoveled the dirt quickly enough to match the pace of the mud that fought to seal the growing hole they were making—Amir from the right and Wilson from the left. She took more steps back as they widened the hole. She nearly fell over trying to avoid being slapped with the dirt from Wilson's shovel. Neither of them noticed where they were discarding the muck.

She turned and scouted the area for Hanem. If he hadn't seen the flare, he had either lost his glasses or gone too far out. She had a nagging feeling that something had happened to him, and that he was hurt. Fog began to settle over them, and her vision was impeded even further. She couldn't see more than a few feet in front of her. It would be impossible to see anyone at all now. It was unlikely that they would even hear him if he called out for help.

A loud thump came from behind her, and she turned

to find that they had jumped into the hole. She knelt and flattened her body onto the earth in an attempt to block the mud raining down on them, but it did little good. Both kept going without pausing, and it was clear that their main intention was not to reach the bottom quickly, but to best each other. It was no less childish now than it was before, but she appreciated that the hostility had finally produced a positive effect.

She heard the sound of metal connecting with wood, and both dropped the shovels. Wilson stepped onto Amir's side, and both fell to their knees to brush the dirt off of what they had found. They stood and shined their flashlights on it. It was a wooden coffin that looked relatively new. It hadn't been underground for very long. After a glance up at her, they pulled the lid open and looked inside.

Amir bent and picked up a small, metal urn. All of them stared at it in surprise, and he threw it up to her. She attempted to catch it but reached too far over the opening. Instead of catching it, she lost her footing and fell into the hole. Before she hit the coffin, Amir caught her, and Wilson caught the urn. Amir let her down gently, and then climbed out of the grave himself. He leaned over and stretched his arm down to her, catching her hand. In one fluid motion, he pulled her up and set her next to him. Wilson found his own way up, and the three of them examined the urn.

She took it and cleaned the dirt off with the inside of her sweater, trying to read the label. When it was finally legible, her heart sank. The name was Dixon Shepherd. She looked across at Wilson, who appeared speechless; his middle name was Dixon, and this was his father.

They all stared at it, at a loss as to what to do. Jezebel handed the urn to Wilson, and he took it without saying a word. They stood together in shocked silence, waiting for something to happen but not knowing what.

Jezebel recovered first and looked at Amir. "Do you know which direction Hanem went in?"

"No."

"Go find him."

"But—"

"We aren't going anywhere, but you are the strongest, and he could be in trouble."

"Do you have another flare gun?"

"No. Where is yours?"

"I dropped it in the mud."

"We won't move. You'll find us again."

He opened his mouth to argue but changed his mind and walked away. She looked back at Wilson, but the expression on his face was unreadable. He seemed too shocked to speak. She waited with him silently, allowing him to have a moment to pull himself together.

Just as he looked up at her, the sounds of a gunshot pierced the air. Something connected with a headstone nearby, breaking it in half. Wilson immediately grabbed her and put her behind him as four more shots were fired. The bullets connected with pieces of stone around them. She fell to her stomach and dragged him down next to her. Her jaw closed on her tongue as she hit the ground. Warm blood filled her mouth, but she spat it out and ignored the pain.

More stones were blown apart, and she got an idea. She crawled back toward the seventh ring, trying to avoid both bullets and pieces of collapsing stone, but it was difficult. Thick pieces of broken granite connected with various areas of her body, a particularly large one falling onto her shoulder and tearing at her skin. She kept going and made it to one of the statues of a centaur. She hid behind it, and Wilson found refuge behind another.

She carefully moved from statue to statue toward a

metal gate that swung violently on its hinges. The car was just beyond it. She cleared three of them before the bust of a dead man was shot, the head sliding off the shoulders and colliding with her head. Her world spun, and she fell over, the rest of the bust falling onto her legs. She squirmed underneath the weight of it and managed to slide from under it by gripping the base of another bust and dragging herself out. The edge where it had broken off dug into the skin of her left calf, and as she pulled herself forward, it created a deep gash from the back of her knee to her ankle.

She heard footsteps draw closer and forced herself to stand. A brief glance behind her showed that Wilson was far away, a large statue of a griffin having fallen on him. In this moment's hesitation, someone grabbed her from behind and covered her mouth. His hot breath invaded her ear as he dragged her backward. She fought to free herself, but his strength overshadowed her own. Instead of allowing him to drag an upright body to whatever destination he had in mind, she dropped herself limply in his arms, forcing a bigger struggle on him due to dead weight.

She took advantage of his momentary hesitation to shift in his grasp and grab onto a nearby statue. He stumbled in surprise but regained his control and tugged her harshly by the waist in order to pry her hands free from the stone. Just before he managed it she let go, causing him to trip, fall onto his back, and release her waist. She collapsed onto the ground, face-planting into the grime. She made to stand up, but he caught hold of her left foot. Pain rang through her leg as the force of his pull triggered a thicker, more consistent stream of blood to gush from her wound.

He regained his balance, and just as he began to drag her away, she turned on her back and dug her fingers into the dirt, slowing down his progress but not deterring him enough to let go. She threw handfuls of dirt at his face, but each time he either dodged it or it came up short. He started laughing and shook his head tauntingly. He looked at the wound on her leg and ran his hands over the gash and stuck three filthy fingers into it. He pushed them roughly through the parts that were deep enough to accommodate him and forcing it to open wider.

The pain was almost blinding, but she refused to give in. Her hand miraculously grazed over something metal, and she recognized it as a shovel. She gripped it tightly, and with every last bit of strength she could muster, she swung it into the cap of his knee. He howled in pain and let go. She stood quickly and slammed the shovel down over his head, forcing him to fall to the ground. She repeated the action two more times for good measure, and then dropped it. She looked around for something heavy and spotted a large statue of an entire person that had been shot out of place. She grabbed it and dragged it as quickly as possible back over to the great brute and pulled the entire thing over his legs. She took a deep breath and rested against two of the headstones behind her.

A burst of headlights blinded her for a few seconds. She blinked the spots in her vision away and recognized the truck that had stormed into the graveyard, blasting the gate off its hinges. Instead of walking toward it, she turned to help Wilson. He was still unconscious on the ground, and before she could take two steps, she stumbled, her leg finally giving out. She dragged herself closer to him on her stomach and caught hold of the stone griffin on top of him. She gritted her teeth and rose to her knees, and then gathered what was left of her strength to push it off of him. It fell over onto another block of granite and broke in half.

She held the top of what was left of the griffin and

tried to pull herself up but was unsuccessful. Her strength had run out, and her body was pulsing with an extreme agony that was too hard to ignore any longer. As someone finally ran over to help her, she caught sight of another dark figure in the distance. He was holding a gun, and it was pointed in her direction.

All movement around her seemed to come to a sudden crashing halt, and seconds later something pierced her chest and sent a toxic shock through her body. There was a blast of light and a burst of sound, and then her world went dark.

<u>SIXTEEN</u>

She stepped into the darkness and let the door slam behind her, cutting her off from all sound. The air was stiflingly hot and humid even at so late an hour. She started down the cracked sidewalk. She walked by locked doors of businesses that had closed at reasonable hours and left passersby to fend for themselves against a haunting darkness that bore an uncomfortable silence.

The street was no different than she typically found it. The gravel road was riddled with holes and bumps that were sure to devastate many a tire, and the sidewalk on both sides was uneven and dusty. The street lamps that sparingly littered the street were either shattered or simply didn't work. She detected nothing out of the ordinary, but there was an unsettling bite to the intense heat of the night air. Everything was as it should have been, but something was wrong.

As she trekked down the side of the road, she abruptly heard footsteps moving at a brisk pace behind her. This was not uncommon. The bar would be closing soon, and customers would surely have to leave. Some of them were not in their right state of minds, but they were harmless. This was a safe town.. Nothing happened here. She inwardly repeated this to herself, attempting to calm her heart rate but failing miserably. She hastened her walk, but whomever was behind her didn't fall behind.

Instead of turning to recognize who it was, she took off down the sidewalk as quickly as she had ever been able to move. All rational thoughts flew from her mind, and she found herself running through the empty, dimly lit, park. No businesses or homes were anywhere near here, but it was a faster route than all of the safer roads. Her only goal was to get out of plain sight as quickly as possible and tearing through the unhealthy brown grass would shave several minutes off of her trip.

About halfway through the open field, the sound of footsteps behind her died away. She slowed down and took a deep breath. She looked behind her, but no one was there. She was completely alone. She turned back to continue on her way and took her usual shortcut through the back alley to her apartment building. She took her time now.

She no longer felt pressured or afraid. She was beginning to think that she had in actuality imagined the entire thing. She hadn't slept in over twenty-four hours, and her head was pounding. She was just paranoid and tired. A crime had not been committed in this town in a very long time, and it was unlikely that the first attack in years would target a waitress.

She walked through the narrow stretch of concrete that was the only divider between the buildings that stood in a small cluster together. She wasn't trying to be quiet anymore. She was almost home.

Without warning, something grabbed her arm and jerked her a few steps back. She turned to find a large man she had never seen before looking down at her with an expression of pure aggression. He was extremely tall and tan, and his green eyes were cold and dead. Before she could speak, he dragged her behind him, not at all fazed by her attempts to wrench herself from his grasp. She tried to scream, but he covered her mouth.

As he pulled her away, she looked desperately for some kind of weapon that would be of service to her. All that was around them were miscellaneous bits of trash on the concrete and bare brick walls that had worn and cracked. Nothing would be of any help to her. She was on her own.

She forced herself to fall over, surprising him and forcing him to loosen his grip. She took the moment of hesitation and took off down the alley again. He shot after her, but she was faster than he was.

She went around a building to her left and sprinted past the side of the structure, trying to make her way to the front and enter the lobby. She cleared the front corner of the building and turned right to face the front steps, finally within reach of actual safety, but the-relief was short-lived. A pair of arms grabbed her aggressively and slammed her against the stone wall to her left. Her head connected with brick violently and she felt liquid spill from the wound and into her hair. She could barely see who was assaulting her, and when the second blow to her pulsing skull came, she lost consciousness completely.

Jezebel's eyes opened, and she sat up. She was sitting in a hospital bed, dressed in a generic white gown and covered with two blankets. Her stomach ached, and the back of her head was throbbing. Her naturally soft skin had turned to goose flesh and she felt chills taking pleasure in resonating throughout her spine. Though the temperature in the room was at a comfortable degree, she was extremely cold.

Someone was talking to her, but she couldn't

recognize who the speaker was, or how many people were in the room. Her world was almost dream-like; those around her were like figments of her imagination—saying only what she willed them to say. They were Shakespearian players in her thoughts, with exits and entrances she herself had created and playing parts that she herself had dreamt up. She knew something was going on around her, but she couldn't comprehend it yet.

An indefinite stretch of time passed, and she swallowed her physical discomfort and sat up. She was in a bed in a large, linoleum-floored room. Across from her was a metal door that led to a bathroom, and to her far left was the exit. On her right was a glass window that looked out onto the brilliant lights of a city. Toy cars roamed the streets below, and small cliques of ants wandered the sidewalks, illuminated by bright lamp posts.

Three wooden chairs lined her bed, and the only other person in the room occupied one of them. It was Hanem, and he was looking at her with a look that clearly expressed he had nothing positive to say. He remained stoic as she took in her surroundings and waited for her to speak. She looked around for Amir, but he wasn't there. She sat up quickly.

"Where's Amir?" she asked.

"I didn't let him come."

"Don't lie to me. What happened to him?"

"Nothing."

"Hanem, what is wrong with him? Is he hurt?"

"He's completely fine, Jezebel."

"Don't try to spare my feelings just because I'm in a hospital bed!"

"I'm NOT! He's FINE!"

"Then where is he?"

"I didn't let him come."

"I don't believe you."

"Do you want to call him and make sure?"

"If I find out that you're lying—"

"I'm not. I really didn't let him come."

"Why did he listen to you?"

"He was unconscious when I brought you to the hospital. Someone hit him in the back of the head. It isn't serious, but I refused to tell him where you are. I didn't think that you would want him here."

"You know me well."

"I've been working for you for a long time."

"How did he take that?"

"Horribly."

"Where is he?"

"I made him stay with Wilson."

"Where?"

"In his car, far away from here."

"He doesn't know I'm in a hospital?"

"I told him you were admitted under a different name, so he would never find you."

"His hatred for you must be quite astronomical right now."

"He has never been fond of me to begin with, regardless."

"Are we going to continue to dance around what you're really waiting to talk about?"

"I am not just here for that."

"Hanem."

"It was his father."

She looked him over more closely. He had gotten banged up badly in the fight. He was sporting seven stitches on his forehead and wore a cast on his right arm. His black hair was disheveled and there was a small cut at the corner of his left eyebrow. His lip was split, and a light scratch lay across his cheek.

"What happened to you?" she asked. "Are you

okay?"

"I'm fine."

"Where were you when we were attacked?"

"I was standing behind the man who shot you."

"Alone?"

"Yes. I was the only one on that side of the cemetery, and the only reason the bullet that hit you was delayed was that I attacked him when he raised the gun. He fired when he thought he had shaken me off, but I caught his arm and knocked it off-center. That is why it hit you in the stomach."

"You saved my life."

"Barely. I didn't catch hold of the gun until the shot was fired, and here you are in a hospital bed."

"Do you remember what he looked like?"

"No, but I managed to keep the gun."

"Where is it?"

Hanem handed it to her, and she immediately recognized it.

"Bugsy's gun," she said. "Was it him?"

"No."

Someone knocked on the door, and Hanem went to open it. A doctor walked in behind him, and he smiled at her. "Looks like you're up."

She didn't return the smile. "Obviously. I'd like to be discharged, now. Bring me the papers."

"We can't do that yet."

"I feel fine."

"That doesn't matter. We ran some tests, and it seems that there was a complication in your test results."

"What kind of complication?"

"You were shot in the chest, just inches above your stomach. We got the bullet out, but there is some scarring."

"Yes, and I'll heal. What's the problem?"

He looked at Hanem. "Are you her husband?"

"Assistant," Hanem said.

"I think you should leave the room then."

"He can stay," Jezebel said.

Hanem got up and pulled the file out of the doctor's hand. He opened it and sat back down.

"Excuse me! That's against hospital policy!" he said.

Hanem ignored him and flipped through the pages. His eyes widened in shock, and it almost fell out of his hand.

"What's wrong with me?" Jezebel asked. "Give it to me. Let me read the damn thing for myself."

He composed himself and handed it to her. She opened it, and her blood ran cold. She read the result over and over, trying to comprehend what she was looking at. It couldn't be possible. She had been so careful.

"This isn't possible," she said.

"I'm sorry if this is an inconvenience for you, but you have to stay another night for close observation. The gunshot wound has made this more dangerous, and I can't let you go."

"I'll be fine."

"You can sign yourself out against hospital recommendations, but that is unsafe. You should stay."

"I'm signing myself out tonight."

"Jezebel—"

"Quiet, Hanem."

"That is up to you, but you should not leave," the doctor said and left.

Jezebel and Hanem sat in silence for a few minutes, both lost in thought. She didn't have time to stay in the hospital any longer. It wasn't a viable option, and she wasn't ready to discuss any of it with Amir. They had more pressing issues to deal with. This could take a backseat for the time being.

"Don't you dare say a word to him, Hanem. I don't want him to know about any of this. Not yet."

"Why not?"

"Because he's going to nag me to see another doctor, and I don't want to deal with this right now."

"Then what are you going to do?"

"Nothing."

"You can't just put yourself in danger because of your pride! You should take better care of yourself when you're in this condition!"

"I'm fine."

"You should stay the night."

"No."

"Leaving here too soon could kill you!"

"Don't be dramatic."

"Just listen to me."

"If I stay another day, he is going to know that something is wrong and come tearing into this hospital like he's on massive doses of methamphetamines. I don't need that problem right now."

"You should tell him."

"It's my body, not his."

"This has nothing to do with that!"

"I don't need his help."

"You're being reckless."

"You shouldn't be shocked."

"Your life is not simply your own."

"I don't want to talk about this, anymore."

"You need help, Jezebel!"

"I'll be fine. I don't need help."

"This is ridiculous."

"Enough. Did Marcel get away?"

"It wasn't him."

"How can you be so sure? You said you didn't see his face. He could have broken out of jail and came after us."

"It could not have been Bugsy Marcel."

"Why?"

Hanem tore out two pages from the file and stuffed them into his pocket. Then, he tossed the rest of it in the trash and got up. He handed her a bag with her clothes inside and put on his jacket.

"Because dead bodies cannot shoot guns," he finally said.

SEVENTEEN

The room was basked in total silence. The sound of breathing was all that could be heard. A small urn was placed on a raised dais at the front of the church. The space was cramped, and the bright white walls were too close to the pews. The entrance to the chapel was enclosed with beautifully stained glass double doors that depicted two royal blue hummingbirds perched in a healthy willow tree.

Each wall held two windows, all of them also built in stained glass and portraying a different scene. They were too big for the walls, but so enthralling was their beauty that the matter of their size was irrelevant. They were mere inches from the ceiling, several feet away from each other, diamond in shape and thick in opacity. They allowed just enough light from the sun to shine through to light up the room without hindrance of a glare.

The first window on the right, closest to the church entrance on this side, was an illustration of a sunset. The color of its fading air was a gentle, pink sea of smoke that tinted the darkening blue sky. The sun was setting into a crashing body of water, the salt-white waves having swallowed half the circumference of its circle and shining against the glass. Even in the bright sunlight that plagued the window, it seemed to glow all on its own.

The window next to it showed the aftermath of the sunset. A wooden ship fought against the dark rising tide. The foremast was broken and hanging limply from the middle of its post and planks of wood were torn apart or simply missing from the visible side of the boat. It was leaning over toward the water, in danger of tipping over, and small outlines of sailors hung on from the edges or had fallen into the sea. The moon was full but was almost covered in its entirety by dark clouds. A crack of lightning had frozen above them, and the emergency raft was in pieces in the water.

The window across from it portrayed a man who lay in a wooden coffin. His eyes were closed, and the expression on his face was somber. It was almost as if he was asleep and dreaming of something that caused him great pain. A woman sat in a chair next to him, covered in black, forehead leaning against the unimpressive box and hand grasping tightly the pale palm of the dead. Tears streaked her cheeks, and her lips formed a long, thin line across the lower half of her face. It was a simple picture, but the pain in it was almost palpable.

The final window was of a woman holding an infant wrapped in a blanket. She was looking down at the baby with joy that contrasted tremendously with the window next to it. Her happiness lit up her fair face, and though her smile was not very wide, her bright green eyes expressed her elation clearly. No one else touched the picture. She was enough.

It was the ceiling that brought the depictions together. A portrait of Christ was painted above, and his hands cradled a dark moon and a bright sun as he lay across the whole ceiling. The backdrop was painted an uncannily loud black color. The meaning was clear: in dark times and light, he was omnipresent, gently taking care of the world and cradling both pain and joy in strong, affectionate arms. It was beautiful enough that it could tender the heart of even the truest nonbeliever.

The people in attendance of the service were few, filling barely two or three pews on only one side. She did not imagine that Wilson had many friends, but she knew nothing of his father. He could have been a decent man, a kind man, or a miserly, intolerable grouch. It was doubtful that anyone here would be honest about his character. He was gone now, and the secrets of who he truly was had joined him. No one spoke ill of the dead.

The minister stood in front of the podium and began to speak, but she tuned his voice out and kept her gaze on Wilson. He was wearing a black suit that he hadn't bothered to iron. His head was in his hands, and his hair was unkempt. It was the first time she saw him as a human being. She had never seen him express any kind of emotion before that moment. It was strange.

Wilson stood and made his way to the podium slowly. He seemed unwilling to go, as if speaking was a feat too difficult for him to manage. At the cemetery, he had been too shocked to react. His father's ashes were handed to him in a jar without warning. There was no time to react then. Now, it looked like the shock had worn off and been replaced with pure pain. His eyebrows were furrowed, and his eyes seemed dim, like he had never smiled a day in his life. The lines on his face were more pronounced, and the bags under his eyes suggested that he hadn't slept in days.

"Dixon Shepherd," he began. "Dixon Shepherd was a father. He was…"

Wilson trailed off, looking at his small white

notecards as if he were seeing them for the first time. He looked at the crowd and then back at the cards. The grief melted away, and all signs of sadness disappeared. The only emotion she could recognize now was anger.

He looked back at the crowd and tore the cards in half, and then in quarters and then in eighths. He tossed them in the direction of his father's urn and watched them fall onto the floor. He turned back to people in the room whose hearts were still beating and started again.

"Dixon Shepherd was a cardiac surgeon. He had a condo in Florida. He had a mansion in Montreal. He had a beach house in California. He had been in the process of buying an island for many years. He spent his entire life worried about nothing but his wealth; constantly looking over bank statements, counting thousands of hundred dollar bills just because he could, and literally trying to swim in a pool of money. He is survived by one son."

Wilson took a deep breath and looked at the ceiling. He hadn't been prepared for this. He looked nervous and angry, as if he was working very hard not to say exactly what was on his mind right then. It couldn't have been appropriate to say out loud or in public.

"A young boy was given all of the material things he could have possibly asked for. He could look at something in a store, or a magazine, or on the damn moon, and it was immediately his. He could ask for anything in the world, and he would not have to work for it. This was what Dixon Shepherd defined as happiness: money and possession. How could anyone not be happy when they can rule the world? He listened to no one. He cared for no one. His love was conditional, and sometimes non-existent. His son lived in his shadow.

He married several times and was faithful to no one. A train of women passed through his house nonstop. His son watched them come and go, asking questions and receiving unsatisfactory answers. Dixon Shepherd taught his son that love was nothing. It meant nothing. It was weakness. It was trivial. It was a sham, and in turn, his son grew up believing the same. The people that came into his life only proved this to be true, and he accepted it. He found no friends. He was alone, always."

Wilson looked down from the ceiling and scanned the hall, finally stopping when his eyes found and held Jezebel's gaze. The more he talked, the more she started to understand him.

"His son grew up searching for something to make him his own person. He wanted to step out of his father's shadow and be part of something else; anything else. He didn't care what it was. He didn't care if it was evil. He didn't care if it was wrong. He didn't care about justice."

He paused and looked at everyone else. "Dixon Shepherd was a philanthropist. He had hosted many benefits, began several charities and even advocated for those who are underprivileged. It is the only good has ever done but let me let you in on a secret: the money he donated was not free. He did absolutely nothing for free. Every penny he gave was given back a different way. Wealth and possessions were his life; he would let none of it go for anyone.

My father was selfish, unkind, unfair, and shallow. He spent his life caring only for his own well-being, and empathy was lost on him. He lived in this world alone, and now he has died alone. No one will miss or remember him. The world will be a better place now that he is gone. The only reason I agreed to do this is that everyone deserves something at the end, even if he is the scum of the earth."

He looked at the urn, as if trying to decide what his

final send-off would be, and then said, "Thank you for everything you did for me, Dixon Shepherd. You are the reason I am the man I am today, but that is nothing to be proud of."

He turned back to the crowd. "I'm sorry that you wasted your day coming here. You are released from whatever obligation that brought you. Just go home. Nothing important is happening here."

With that, he stepped off the stage and left without looking back. Jezebel stood and followed him out, leaving Amir and Hanem behind. Neither of them made a move to come after her.

Jezebel went through the back doors of the church and looked around the small patch of healthy grass. There was very little room for anything aside from shrubs that lined the chain-link fence that divided the property from the houses on either side. There were several benches and a red slide for children, as well as two swings that were far too small for an adult to sit on.

Wilson had taken a seat on the bench just left of the door, his elbows resting on his knees and his head hanging. She looked at him for a long moment, and then joined him. There was a short silence, and then he opened his mouth to speak.

"Did your bodyguard see you come out here after me?"

"Don't be condescending."

"His jealousy is obnoxious."

"Why do you hate him so much?"

He took off his suit jacket and then sat back against the dirty bench. She waited for him to say something, and a couple of quiet minutes later, he finally said, "He reminds me too much of someone I hate."

"And who is that?"

"The man I just ranted about."

"Your father?"

"Yes."

"How?"

"Is he Persian?"

"Yes."

"My father was also Persian."

"That's racist, and it's not a legitimate reason."

He shrugged and didn't say anything.

"Amir isn't jealous," she said.

"Then why doesn't he like me?"

"He doesn't trust you. None of us do. You are a police officer."

"Why do you care, if you aren't criminals?"

"I'm not having this out with you here."

"Are you—"

"Bugsy Marcel is dead."

Wilson's eyes widened. "What?"

"His body was buried in New York three days ago."

"How?"

"One of the guards was sent to let him out, but the cell door opened on his corpse."

"Suicide?"

"Murder-suicide."

"He killed another inmate, and then killed himself?"

"Allegedly."

"Is that what the report said?"

"Yes."

"Were there details?"

"Of course there weren't."

"You don't believe them?"

"You know that I'm a skeptic."

"What do you think really happened then?"

"I don't know, but nothing is ever as it seems. Who gave you the Athena Elias file?"

"You're asking me about this now?"

"You would rather talk about that horrible display of yours?"

"The man deserved it."

"We do not speak ill of the dead."

"I do not want to talk about this with you."

"Then answer the question."

"I stole it," he said.

"From?"

"They were talking about it at the precinct, and I took it off the new chief's desk when he wasn't looking."

"But why that one in particular?"

"It was an unsolved disappearance with no leads. What could possibly attract me more?"

"You work in New York City. There's violent crime going on in every nook and cranny here."

"I am not lying."

"Something doesn't make sense."

"What?"

"I haven't figured it out yet."

"Then your accusations are unfounded."

"All of my accusations are unfounded until people are stupid enough to prove them right."

"You are one of the most arrogant people I have ever met."

"You are no different."

"You're insulting me at my father's funeral."

"You clearly don't give a damn."

"Do you think he was involved?"

She avoided the question. "Isn't the Elias case out of your precinct's jurisdiction?"

"Yes."

"Then why did yours have it?"

"I really do not know."

"Do you know which precinct it belonged to?"

"Yes."

"Have you been inside it?"

"Yes."

"Good."

"I'll show you how to get inside."

She didn't say anything.

"If you have something to say, say it, Jezebel."

"Today isn't the best day."

"I don't care."

"Why are you helping me, Asher?"

"I'm not helping you. I'm helping myself. You're a means to an end. I'm sorry if that upsets you."

"It doesn't."

"I told you. We are more alike than I thought we were."

She laughed a little. "You're not really going to keep me out of this investigation."

"No, I'm not."

He stood to leave, but turned back to her and said, "You called me by my first name."

"Does it matter?"

"Just an observation."

"I wouldn't get used to it."

"He wouldn't like it."

She almost laughed. "Goodbye, Shepherd."

"That is not funny."

"That's a matter of opinion."

He walked away, leaving her outside by herself. She had no intention of going to the cemetery with him. A few minutes later, Amir came out and sat next to her. Neither of them said anything. He pulled out a cigarette and lit it. She moved a few inches away from him, but he didn't ask questions or react. He took a drag and blew the smoke in a different direction.

"You didn't have to come, today," she finally said.

"Why are you so quiet? What's wrong?"

She took the cigarette out of his hand and threw it on the ground. He stepped on it to put it out.

"Something showed in my lab results, when I was

taken to the hospital a few days ago."

"Are you sick?"

"In a manner of speaking."

"What does that mean?"

She looked at him. "I'm pregnant."

She got up and walked away. He just stared after her.

EIGHTEEN

Jezebel avoided Amir completely, and he didn't try to force her to talk about it. She had no idea what his take on the situation was, and she preferred to ignore it for the time-being. It was an unhealthy way to go about it, but she wasn't ready to bring it into her reality yet. She had more pressing issues to deal with, and though Amir was giving her space, his patience would run out eventually. She decided to wait until he couldn't take it anymore.

Wilson had refused to take a break to recover from his father's death. He insisted that death was a natural occurrence, and he had hated his father too much to interrupt his life. Jezebel hadn't tried to push him or talk about it. They just moved on to decide what to do next.

No one was stupid enough to suggest that they break into the police station itself. It was dangerous, foolish, and short-sighted. Very few places in New York were as heavily secured as police precincts. The only way to gain a safe access was to hide in plain sight.

The police station was busier than she had believed it would be at so late an hour. It was also bigger than the one she had visited to see Wilson. She sat before a clean, metal desk, waiting for an officer to join her.

In front of other desks in the room sat Amir and three other men. Hanem could not be seen, as it was common knowledge that he worked with her. It would be suspicious if he had come to report a different crime than her at the same time, and so he sent three of his men to take his place and joined Adel outside. Each of them, including herself, were there to report a minor crime they witnessed in the area. Wilson was speaking to the chief of the department, distracting him from recognizing Jezebel and making a big to do of her presence.

An old, sleep-deprived officer sat behind the desk in front of her. The smiled on his face was small, but polite.

"How can I help you, Miss White?" he asked.

"I am here to report a sexual assault."

His eyebrows shot up. "Excuse me?"

"I was walking to my car from a function just a few hours ago, and I saw a man attack a young girl from behind. He ran away when he heard me yell, and so did she. I think that she may be too afraid to report it."

"Did you see the victim?"

"Yes."

"Did you recognize her?"

"No."

"Unfortunately, there is not much that I can do unless the victim reports it herself."

"Nothing at all?"

"Unless you can find her and convince her to come forward, this is out of my hands."

"She won't come forward on her own."

"That is her choice to make."

She sighed and stood. "Thank you for—"

All light was suddenly cut off, and the building was

drenched in total darkness. There was shouting coming from down the hall, and the officer got up and ran toward the noise, as did everyone else in the room. She felt someone put a set of keys in her hand, and she walked in the direction of the door she had made note of before. It was the chief's office, and she unlocked it quickly. Wilson came up behind her.

"Ready?" he asked.

"Do you know how long we have?"

"We have exactly ten minutes before the generators turn the electricity back on," he said.

"I can work with that."

She opened the door and walked in, Wilson closing the door and the blinds behind them. She pulled a flashlight out of her bag and scanned the room. It was among the most lackluster offices she had ever seen. There was nothing but a small file cabinet and thick, mahogany desk with a chair behind it. It was the only seat in the room. The white walls were bare, and the carpet was a beaten gray. The office was relatively clean, save for the small black trash bin that was slightly overflowing with crumpled paper and food containers.

Jezebel immediately walked behind the desk and Wilson took the file cabinet. Both dropped to their knees, but when she attempted to open the last drawer, it was locked.

"Key," she said to Wilson.

He threw a ring of keys to her and went back to the cabinet. She tried four different keys before finally finding one that fit into the lock. She pulled out the drawer and found a stack of files. She went through them quickly, looking for the one name that would in some way pull the entire debacle together, knowing that her ten minutes were quickly running out. Seconds into her search, she stopped at one name that was extremely familiar: Jezebel White.

She pulled it out and began to stuff it into her bag when something cold was jammed against the back of her head. She didn't have to turn to know that it was a gun. She saw Wilson stand very slowly, hands up. He looked confused at the face of whoever the assailant was.

"Get up," the man behind her said. She immediately recognized the voice but made no attempt to get away from him. She stood carefully, but she didn't put her hands up.

"Turn," he said.

Jezebel turned and looked up at him.

It was the same person who had accosted her in her home without an invitation. Even in the feeble beam of her misdirected flashlight, she saw a sneer radiating from his pudgy, disgusting face. His mouth was parted widely, and his yellowing teeth seemed to glow in the dark. His black hair was combed back, matted heavily with several coats of hair product.

The man's wide girth seemed to have grown; it took enough space that the area between them was less than two feet, even with his back nearly glued to the wall behind him. Though he had done minimal work since he had stepped into the office, he was sweating profusely and barely catching his breath. He was blowing hot air in her face with each exhale.

"No less disgusting than usual then, Lanyard," Jezebel said.

He hit the side of her head with the gun violently. She was slightly shaken but didn't visibly react.

"Watch how you talk to me," he snapped.

"I don't take orders."

"You'll do what I tell you."

She crossed her arms. "So, it was you."

"What exactly are you blaming me for?"

"You've been trying to frame me."

"You are the most paranoid woman alive, White."

"Why did you do it?"

"I don't know what you're on about."

"Why are you *after me?*"

"You shouldn't be part of this business. You are not one of us. You should have no power, and you're interrupting the system with your intent on picking and choosing cargo."

"Cargo."

"Yes, cargo."

"You went through all of this trouble just to end my career? How boring has your life become, Lanyard?"

"I'd think you'd be smarter than to talk down to me when I have a gun to your head."

"I didn't know you could think."

"Your mouth is going to get you murdered."

"Is that meant to scare me?"

"You are just a fragile woman who doesn't know her place."

"And women belong in the home?"

"In the bedroom."

"I was under the impression that you prefer men, Lanyard."

He slapped her with the back of his hand. "Shut up."

"No."

"You're so proud and egotistical that you would jeopardize your own life just to save face?"

"Yes, I am."

"What are you doing in the chief's office?" Wilson asked.

"I am the new chief."

"I have never heard of you."

"You're hardly the most knowledgeable on this force."

"Someone your size would be hard not to notice."

"Careful how you talk to me, Wilson."

"Don't hurt her."

"I am now your commanding officer. If you value your job, do not tell me what to do."

"I've seen no evidence of that. Let her go."

"Why are you so interested in what happens to her?"

"Because this is my investigation, and you won't ruin it for me."

Lanyard laughed. "Are you that terrible of a detective that you have yet to figure out what she is?"

"It doesn't matter. If you want to hurt someone, hurt me. I am the one who betrayed the department."

"Perhaps we should use this time to get to know each other better," Lanyard said. "Let me help you with your investigation. Give him the file you were trying to steal, White."

Jezebel neither spoke nor moved.

Lanyard knocked the firearm into her head again, this time with more force. She blinked away the pain but didn't react. He tried again, and she almost fell over, but she still didn't open her mouth.

"GIVE IT TO HIM!"

"No."

"I *will* kill you."

"Do it."

Lanyard snatched the file from her and handed it to the other detective, but Wilson didn't open it.

"Let go of her, I said."

"I'll just tell you what's in that file, if you aren't enough of a man to look at it yourself."

"Why do you want me to hate her?"

"Because she deserves it. She is a monster."

"If you are willing to take a life, so are you."

Lanyard laughed mirthlessly. "You have been after solving the Athena Elias case for a long time."

"That case was closed. Bugsy Marcel killed her. I already proved that."

"Yes, he did."

"Then leave her alone. She didn't kill her."

"You are investigating more than just Elias's disappearance, Wilson. Would you like me to solve the entire puzzle for you?"

"No."

Lanyard ignored him. "She was behind other disappearances, and had planned to take Elias, as well. Bugsy simply got to her first."

"She killed them?"

"No, she is not a killer."

"How do you know any of this?"

"I know a lot of things."

"Why do you have a gun to her head then, if she's not a killer?"

"*She* is not a killer. I never said that I am not."

"Why are you admitting this openly?"

"Because no one will believe you."

"What are you telling me? You said she isn't a killer!"

"She sells them down the river for profit, my friend."

"I don't understand."

"Women are expensive. They could easily fund a mansion."

There was a heavy silence then. Wilson looked as though he was struggling to come up with a response. He opened his mouth and closed it several times, like a fish gasping for breath out of water.

"Is that true, Jezebel?" he asked.

She didn't respond.

"Is it true?"

She just looked at him.

"SAY SOMETHING!"

"Don't tell me what to do, Wilson."

"If you tell me that this is not true, I will burn the file."

Amir had entered the room. She couldn't see or hear him, but he had snuck in somehow. She needed to stall just a little bit longer, but she couldn't think clearly. Lanyard was breathing heavily in her hear, and Wilson was waiting for her to help him come to terms with what was happening.

"No, you won't," she said.

Lanyard hit her with the gun again. She stumbled and hit her head on the corner of the desk. Amir was hiding under it, holding piece of metal. She quickly averted her eyes to keep Lanyard from looking in the same direction. A moment later, Lanyard grabbed her arm and dragged her back to her feet.

"Watch how you speak to him," Lanyard said.

"I don't need you to defend me," Wilson said.

"You no longer have a logical reason to defend her," Lanyard said. "If she denies anything I'm saying, I'll concede."

"Jezebel, I won't ask you again," Wilson said.

She crossed her arms, but still didn't answer him. Her eyes darted around the room, trying to find something that she could grab the second Amir made his first move. There was a wooden bat in the corner of the room, but it was too far away for her to get to it before Wilson.

"Silence is tacit compliance, you know," Lanyard said.

"I'm not going to bear witness against myself," Jezebel finally said.

"So it's true."

"I didn't say that."

"You look so upset," Lanyard said. "Isn't she the very same woman you had been stalking because you wanted to toss her in jail?"

"That is none of your business."

"You've finally solved your case. You should be thanking me."

"I didn't want it like this."

"You took too long. You f—"

Lanyard was cut off mid-sentence by something connecting with the back of his head in the darkness. He let out a muffled groan and dropped his gun. She quickly picked it up and pointed it at his head. He looked up and started laughing, his bundles of fat shaking with every guffaw. Amir stepped out of the darkness but didn't say anything. He just waited for her to react. Wilson hadn't taken a step.

"You won't shoot," Lanyard said.

"Yes, I will."

"Do it."

She cocked the gun. "Don't tempt me."

"You're too weak."

"You don't know what I'm capable of."

He laughed and reached under a desk. He detached a gun and pointed it back at her. Amir grabbed him, and they started struggling. Lanyard fell to the floor and pointed his gun at Amir. He rested his finger on the trigger.

"NO!" she yelled.

Without stopping to think about it, she pulled the trigger on the gun in her hand. A silent bullet connected with Lanyard's skull, and he fell over. Blood seeped from the wound, and light left his eyes. The gun fell out of her hand limply, but she couldn't take her eyes off of him.

Amir looked between the only other conscious people in the room. Wilson looked from the body to Jezebel, and then back again.

"I killed him," she said. She had willingly murdered

someone in cold blood. No one had forced her to do this, and she hadn't even hesitated first. She felt like she couldn't breathe.

"To save my life," Amir said.

"Did you do it, Jezebel?" Wilson asked.

"I killed him," she repeated.

"That isn't what I'm asking you about."

She didn't say another word, and the detective's face fell. What Lanyard had said was true, and he had no idea how to react. She watched him, waiting in silence for his final verdict.

He took a deep breath. "I will create another distraction so that you can leave without arousing suspicion. Leave Lanyard to me and just go. I'll take care of it. I'll make sure that it can't be traced back to you."

"You won't arrest her?" Amir asked.

"No."

"You said you weren't going to keep her out of your investigation."

"I didn't want it like this. Take her and go."

Amir nudged Jezebel, but she didn't move. She couldn't take her eyes off of the body at her feet.

"Is he really dead?" she asked.

Wilson knelt hesitantly and felt for a pulse on Lanyard's neck, despite the obvious fatality of the gunshot wound. After a few seconds of trying to find the right spot, he gave up and stood.

"Yes, he's dead."

"I killed him," Jezebel said.

"Out of defense," Amir said. "You are not a killer."

"I am now."

Someone tried to open the door, but it was locked. The person knocked, but none of them made a move to open it. Whoever it was didn't relent. He kept knocking and trying the knob. He was yelling something, but the door was too thick for them to hear him.

"Pull him behind the desk," Wilson said.

Amir picked Lanyard up and shoved him roughly under the desk. The entire body didn't fit, but he was out of sight. Wilson opened the door, and the police officer she had been speaking to was standing there, trying to catch his breath.

"Where's the chief?" he asked.

"He went to check on the noise and left us in here," Wilson said. "Is something wrong?"

"Wanted to report to him."

"Check outside again."

The man left, and Wilson looked back at Jezebel. "Leave quickly. I will take care of it."

He left the room, leaving the file on the floor at her feet. She picked it up and stuffed it into the handbag she had brought with her. She took one last look at Lanyard's lifeless body and picked up the gun he had been holding.

She handed it to Amir. "Take the other one, too."

"Okay," Amir said.

NINETEEN

Days passed, and Jezebel had thrown herself into her work, ignoring Hanem and Amir entirely. Both men continuously nagged her to take a break. They forced food down her throat when they felt she wasn't eating and walked in and out of her office to interrupt her work. Hanem canceled clients and held her calls, while Amir took papers away from her when she wouldn't stop to rest.

Hanem and Amir did not—and would never—like one another, but they endured each other's presence long enough to develop several elaborate plans to compel her to rest. She dismissed them all immediately, each time responding with backhanded and often patronizing compliments on their teamwork. No matter how hard she tried to annoy them, they refused to stop.

Three weeks passed, and their pestering became increasingly irritating, but nothing she said stopped them. Finally, Jezebel did something that they would both absolutely hate her for: she locked them together in a room. There were no secret exits or entrances, and to add insult to injury, she had hidden the key somewhere inside with them.

Hanem had been in his study and Amir out doing something he had chosen not to tell her about when they received her call. She said nothing to either about the other, only telling them to meet her in the far east living room of the house. Neither man asked questions.

When they arrived, she was nowhere to be found. All that was in the room was a note pinned on the inside of the door:

I would advise you not to pester me again. The key is in the room. I will not let you out. You both think that you are so smart, and if that's true, you will find your own way out. If you really know me as well as you claim you do, you will know exactly where I hid it.

Take the time to enjoy each other's company while you look. I know how fond you are of each other.

It was too condescending a note for Amir to use brute strength to force their way through. She had asked Adel to close the door as soon as both of them had entered. She had specifically wanted him to do it, because nothing would irritate Amir more than being locked up by his own brother and being unable to cause him any kind of pain as revenge. Like Amir, Adel did as he was told regardless of what was asked of him, so long as she was not ordering him to spill the blood of the few he cared about. Amir was one of those people, but because he knew that she would never hurt him, he followed her orders to the letter and locked his brother's cage.

After she heard them begin yelling out for her and at each other, she returned to her study to continue working. She was in a good mood as she worked. She hoped that they would tear each other apart so deeply that they would hate each other too much to collaborate ever again, no matter the reason. It would be easier to ignore them if they were a divided front.

A few hours passed, and she was finally about halfway through the stack of files she had been reviewing. Her satisfaction had not yet faded, but when she read the name in the file in front of her, the smirk she wore disappeared.

"Athena Elias?"

"Present."

Jezebel looked up, and before her stood a young woman who very closely resembled a girl by the same name who was murdered in cold blood, or so she had been told.

"Athena Elias," Jezebel repeated.

The girl sat in the chair in front of her and crossed her arms. "Sound familiar, Dr. White?"

The girl did look remarkably like the Athena Elias that she had seen, but at closer look, there were many differences. This one had much thinner lips, and her eyes were wider. Her hair was a lighter shade of brown, and her face was clear of any sign of acne. Her teeth were also straighter and whiter. Her mouth was made for a smirk. It didn't seem like she smiled often. She was also thinner, her body having smaller curves, perhaps due to intentional lack of eating.

"How did you get in here?" Jezebel asked.

"The maid let me in."

"Which one?"

"Don't pretend you know their names."

"Answer me."

"No," she said simply.

"Worried about their jobs?"

"Worried about annoying you."

"Who are you?"

She leaned back and balanced her chair on its back legs. "Not the dead girl. Don't worry."

"That's not what I asked you."

"I'm the dead girl's sister."

"By the same name."

"Yes."

"Why are you here?"

"Court-mandated."

"And you thought a good time to see me would be after my office hours have ended and inside my home?"

"As good a time as any."

"Get out."

"Oh, aren't you just a little bit curious?"

"No. Get out."

"Liar, liar."

Jezebel gritted her teeth. "Why are you here?"

"I told you why."

"What did you do?"

"The file is in your hand."

"Answer the question."

"Nothing serious."

"That isn't what I asked you."

"I hit my boyfriend."

Jezebel opened the file and looked over her previous charges. She had been arrested for drug possession twice in the past, but she was fined and released. This time, she was charged with pulling a knife on a man she was living with and attempting to assault him but had not managed to touch him more than once, and not fatally.

"Drug possession," Jezebel said.

"Thought that one would pique your interest."

"And why would you think that?"

"Athena wasn't drugging me, if that's what you're thinking."

"Make your point."

"Cops caught me on a good day."

"You didn't have enough illegal substances to prove

intent to sell."

"Yes."

"Runs in the family then."

"Love of money runs in the human race, not just my family."

"Maybe, but not everyone in the human race profits from ruining the lives of children."

"I didn't say that I deal to kids."

"You didn't have to."

"Very astute."

"Are you currently dealing?"

"Maybe."

"Why are you telling me? I could report you."

"Patient-therapist confidentiality."

"That stops at felonies."

"Not past ones."

"You seem so sure."

"I am a lawyer."

Jezebel was taken aback. "Excuse me?"

The girl laughed. "Yes, I am a licensed lawyer in the state of New York. It's surprising, I know."

"Then why turn to drugs?"

"Had to make ends meet. Couldn't find a job, and I was not about to sink so low that I would become a janitor."

"But dealing drugs is classier."

"Of course."

Jezebel tossed the file back onto the desk. "These papers are fake. Why did you really come here?"

"They are not—"

"This was a very poor attempt at imitating legal documents that you are fully aware I see every day. I would expect more from a licensed lawyer. Why the hell are you in my house?"

"I want to know what my sister said to you when you saw her."

"Why would I tell you that?"

"Because she's dead now."

"That's confidential."

"She's dead, anyway."

"I cannot share that information."

"Just tell me what she said."

"Tell me what you really want from me."

"I told you what I want."

"Liar."

The smirk fell off of her face, and all signs of condescending amusement were gone. "You killed her."

"Excuse me?"

"You heard me."

"The man who killed her is dead."

"Murdered, you mean."

"He took his own life."

"I don't believe that."

"There isn't very much for me to do about your wild imagination, even if I cared about it. I'm sorry for your loss."

"Tell me why you killed my sister."

"Who sent you to me?"

The girl ignored the question. "I don't believe that Uncle Bugsy would kill his own niece."

"Excuse me?"

"Oh, you weren't aware that Athena and I are his sister's daughters? Not very thorough of you, Doctor."

"Martha had no children."

"But Melena did."

"He had another sister?"

"Adoptive, but yes."

"What is your real name?"

"Annie Elias."

"Well, Annie Elias, this would not be the first time a man has killed a member of his own family. Your sister was drugging Martha. Marcel was clearly playing favorites with his siblings."

"I don't believe you."

"What could I possibly have to do with any of it?"

"You were under investigation for her murder."

"That does not mean that I am guilty."

"You are the last link."

Jezebel paused and leaned forward. "When did Bugsy finally meet you, Annie Elias?"

"Excuse me?"

"Bugsy Marcel didn't have a clue that she was his niece when he killed her, did he?"

The girl hesitated. "Where are you getting that from?"

"He had no idea what Melena's children looked like, because he hadn't seen her in years."

"How could you possibly know that?"

"Because Bugsy Marcel has never once visited Greece, which is where you and your sister were born."

She hesitated. "You have no idea where he has or hasn't been."

"Has he been to Greece?"

"Yes."

"You don't sound very sure."

"That doesn't matter! I want to know who killed my uncle!"

"I thought you were here to ask about your sister."

The girl blanched. "I am."

"I have just one more question."

"I won't tell you who sent me to you."

"Did your mother leave you and your sister in Greece after you were born?"

Shock flitted across her features. "N-No."

"You're lying to a psychologist."

"How-How did you know that?"

Jezebel sat back in her chair. "I had nothing to do with either death. I would have been arrested for at least one of them. The law enforcement in this state is diligent enough to have had me convicted and spending my days in a cell by now. Get out of my office, before I call the police. You have overstayed your welcome."

The girl got up quickly and left. She slammed the door behind her, leaving Jezebel alone with her thoughts. The pieces were slowly falling into place, and the picture was turning out far worse than she had believed it would. It was becoming very clear that she was guilty of crimes she hadn't realized she had committed. Though she had gotten accustomed to the fact that she was a criminal, being blindsided by a heinous act of this kind shook her.

The Elias sisters were not placed in her life by chance. There was a reason, and it was undoubtedly something terrible. She was beginning to question whether she really wanted to know the truth or not. Sometimes it was better to stay ignorant.

Not two minutes later, Hanem and Amir charged in, both looking extremely angry.

"THAT WAS NOT FUNNY!" they yelled.

"Do not yell at me."

The two men deflated upon noticing the expression on her face. All signs of anger were replaced with worry.

"Is everything alright?" Hanem asked.

"Yes. Leave."

"What's wrong?" Amir asked.

"Nothing. Go away."

"Your attempt to make us hate each other too much to nag you failed," Hanem said. "And after that stunt, any chance you had of getting rid of us is long gone. What is going on, Jezebel?"

She didn't respond, choosing instead to lean back in her chair and focus on the ceiling.

"Don't ignore us," Amir said.

She was lost in thought, pretending they weren't there. The girl who had just left was Athena Elias's sister. Someone had filled her head with lies and sent her after Jezebel. It couldn't have been Lanyard. Lanyard was dead.

"We won't go away," Hanem said.

"You can't ignore us forever," Amir said.

"And the longer you keep this up, the more you will have to tolerate us," Hanem said.

"Tell us what happened," Amir said.

She finally looked at them. "Don't tell me what to do."

"Tell us what happened," he repeated.

"Learn to ask nicer, and maybe I will change my mind."

"Fine. *Please*."

"That's better. Now get out."

"Tell us."

"I need to make sense of this before I create wild theories with nothing but circumstantial evidence to back up my claims."

"And we can help you do that."

"Did you just validate Hanem as a legitimate form of help?"

"You can try to keep distracting me, but it will not make me stop asking questions or go away."

She sighed. "My mother was Greek, Amir."

TWENTY

Hanem and Amir sat in the seats in front of her. Hanem seemed to have worked it out already but waited for her to say it out loud.

"What does that matter?" Amir asked.

"Did you see a girl leaving as you walked in?" Jezebel asked.

"Yes. Who was she?"

"Annie Elias."

"Any relation to Athena Elias?"

"Twin sister."

"What did she want?" Hanem asked.

"She accused me of killing her sister."

"Did she say who sent her?" Hanem asked.

"No."

"You look upset," Amir said.

Jezebel furrowed her eyebrows. "Their mother's name was Melena. *My* mother's name was Melena."

"What are you getting at, Jezebel?" Amir asked.

"When I was five years old, my mother left me to care for her mother in Greece. She took Lionel and left me with my father, and she did not come back until one year later, on my sixth birthday."

"You don't actually think that they are your sisters?" Amir asked.

"Both of them are exactly six years younger than me, Amir."

"That is completely circumstantial, Jezebel! It means nothing!"

Hanem shook his head. "It makes sense. Jezebel was set up to see Athena assaulting a girl in the park. She was never a patient. I never saw her anywhere near the office."

"And you think that someone brought her into your life as revenge?" Amir asked.

"Her mother is Bugsy's adoptive sister."

"Didn't they say that Athena was their cousin?" Hanem asked.

"Yes, but she wasn't."

"Why would they lie?" Amir asked.

"I don't know, but I don't think he knew that she was his niece when he murdered her."

"You are trying to tell us that Bugsy Marcel was your *uncle?*" Amir asked.

"Someone set me up to harm my own sister, but I sincerely doubt that it was Marcel."

"Who sent that girl to you?" Hanem asked.

"She refused to tell me."

"What are you—"

Amir was cut off by a shrill scream and the sound of gunshots somewhere inside the house. The three of them shot out of the office and swiftly descended the stairs. They followed the sound of people shouting through the east living room and into the foyer. There, gracing the floor in all her glory, was Annic Elias. She lay in a crumpled heap, multiple gunshot wounds pouring rivers of blood from her abdomen, chest, and left leg to ruin the red parquet.

There was pure terror reflected in her eyes, as if her assailant still stood before her. Her lips were parted slightly, and a trickle of blood had fallen from her nose. Though the life had only just left her body, her pale skin seemed lucid, echoing the bright light that illuminated the hall.

The door was still wide open, but the shooter was no longer in sight. She went up the three steps and stood at its threshold. A black sedan was making its escape far off in the distance. The windows had been tinted to hide who was inside, and the license plate had been covered. He left no trace of his identity behind. It was a perfectly executed crime.

Adel and four maids were standing there, the former irately attempting to calm the weeping women in the room. Adel was not a patient man, but his explosive temper was nowhere to be found. He was awkwardly patting the women on the shoulders and mumbling.

"QUIET!" Amir yelled.

Everyone present fell into silence and turned to wait for Jezebel to speak. She cleared her throat.

"Find someone willing to take the fall for this, and then call the police, Adel," she said.

Adel nodded and left. She turned to Amir. "I want everyone out of my house immediately. Make sure that there is absolutely no one left. I don't care how you have to do it. Just do it quickly."

"Alright."

She looked at Hanem. "How long will it take you to get the security footage from all of the cameras?"

"Ten minutes."

"Go."

She pointed to the four remaining maids and motioned for them to follow her into the kitchen. They obediently walked in, keeping their panic at bay in fear of Jezebel's reaction to their hysteria.

"Sit," she said.

They all sat.

"What happened?"

The youngest of the four, a teenaged girl with blonde hair and multiple piercings in each ear, blinked away the tears in her eyes and raised her hand. The rest were too timid to open their mouths at all.

"This isn't a classroom. Speak."

"We were all sitting in here waiting for the food to finish cooking, and there was a loud banging sound outside of the door," the girl said.

"And you saw nothing?" Jezebel asked.

"We ran out just as the man who shot her was leaving."

"And you didn't follow?"

"He had a gun!"

"What did he look like?"

"He was covered in all black. Even his face."

"You remember nothing at all about him?"

They all shook their heads.

"How big was he?"

"Tall and thin," the eldest maid said. Her voice was the weakest of them, but she was the only one who hadn't been in tears.

"Did any of you touch the body?"

"No."

"Listen to me very carefully," Jezebel said. "I want you to leave here and not come back for two days. You saw nothing. You heard nothing. This did not happen, as far as you are concerned. Go through the back door, and do not even *look* at the body. Is that clear?"

"But what about—"

Jezebel cut the teenager off. "This is for your own protection, not mine. If you want to be suspected of murder in the first degree, feel free to stay. I won't stop you, but you've been warned."

"Thank you," the older woman said.

"You're welcome. Go."

They vacated their chairs and left the kitchen. Jezebel returned to her office, not bothering to spare a glance at the girl covered in blood in her foyer. She had already seen enough to give her nightmares.

Five minutes passed, and Hanem entered the room holding a disc. He inserted it into the computer on her desk and clicked a file. He typed in a password and opened the footage from the camera in the hallway. He stopped it at the appropriate time frame, and then leaned on the left side of the desk to watch it with her.

One of the maids opened the front door and stumbled back. An exceptionally tall man holding a gun pushed her to the floor and stepped over her. He was Caucasian, but he was dressed entirely in black. He was wearing a face mask and gloves; nothing of his identity was at all discernable, save for the eyes. He had bright green eyes.

Two of the other maids ran out of the kitchen and cried out at the sight of the trespasser. He motioned for them to be quiet with his right index finger, and then turned to walk deeper into the house. He saw the small camera on the ceiling and pointed his weapon toward it. His finger rested on the trigger, and a moment later, the screen went dark.

They watched the footage twice more, and finally, she noticed something that gave him away.

"Stop," she said.

"Do you see something?" Hanem asked.

"Look at his wrist."

For less than three seconds, the man's jacket sleeve had hiked up just far enough to reveal part of a very familiar tattoo.

"A snake tattoo?" Hanem asked.

"A cobra."

"Does it look familiar?"

"That is Michael Saint's wrist, Hanem."

"You think Michael Saint shot her."

"Unless he lent his wrist to someone else, yes."

Amir walked into the office and asked, "Do you recognize him?"

"She says it was Michael Saint," Hanem said.

"Do *not* talk about me as if I'm not here," Jezebel said.

"You think Michael Saint broke into your house and murdered Annie Elias?" Amir asked.

"Yes."

"That is so far-fetched, Jezebel."

"Has anything about this situation been anything but?"

"Fair."

"Did Adel find someone?" Hanem asked.

"Yes. He's planting the evidence now. He said he'll be done in about an hour, and then he'll call the police."

"Why was your brother in the foyer, Amir?" Jezebel asked.

Amir shifted uncomfortably. "I don't know."

"Do not lie again."

He sighed. "He is in a relationship with one of the maids."

"The blonde one," Jezebel said.

"How did you know?"

"He was very gentle with that one when she was wailing in his ear. Why is he hiding it?"

"Adel is far too proud to let anyone find out that he is dating a maid," Hanem said.

"I don't need distracted people working for me."

"He isn't distracted," Amir said. "Everyone on your payroll is dating someone. Don't be unfair to my brother."

"I'm not."

"You're taking your irritation with me out on him. Please don't."

She ignored him.

"Send the police up to me when they get here. Amir, find out where Saint is right now, and Hanem, go watch Adel."

They left, and she sat back in her chair to think. There were so many factors, but what disturbed her the most was that three of her siblings had now been murdered in cold blood because of her. They would be alive, had she not been their sister. She vaguely tried to remember if her mother had ever mentioned them before.

A teenaged girl sat on a thinly carpeted floor, wrapped in a slightly tattered blanket and holding a book she had read about four times. A cold, foreboding chill dominated the night air. Everything was still. Nothing could be heard aside from the senseless mumbles of the only other person in the room: a woman whose brain had become addled with grief.

The woman was holding a mirror, not seeming at all bothered by her disheveled appearance. Her hair fell in tangled, unruly knots around her face, and the clothes she had been wearing for days were torn and frayed. Her green eyes had not lost the cheerful spark they had before her life went sour, but it was different. There was madness in it now. The grin she wore was almost maniacal.

The girl had gotten used to the woman's whispers. It had become far easier to tune them out over time. On this particular night, however, it was impossible to ignore. The woman was louder and more coherent than usual. The way she stared at her own reflection while she spoke was unnerving.

"They have my eyes," the woman mumbled. "My

eyes."

She chose not to answer.

The woman put the mirror down. "You have your father's eyes."

"My father's eyes are brown."

The woman lifted the mirror again and repeated, "They have my eyes."

"Who?"

The woman's face melted into irritation. "They have my eyes."

The girl shook her head and went back to the book, but the woman seemed to have had enough. She threw the mirror against the wall, and it shattered, shards scattering all over the floor.

"Listen to what I am saying!" the woman said angrily.

"No," the girl said and stood, letting the blanket fall around her feet. She went to a medicine cabinet, took a bottle of small, white capsules, and returned to stand in front of the woman. The girl tossed them into her lap, took her book and blanket, and sat in the window. Instead of continuing to read, she closed her eyes and fell asleep.

Some time later, a loud thud woke her. She sat up quickly and found that the woman had fallen to the floor with the open bottle limply in her hand.

"Jezebel!"

She blinked and looked up. It was Wilson. He looked like he hadn't slept in years. His face was pale, and there were dark circles around his eyes. His eyes were dimmer than usual, and it looked like he had stopped caring about what he looked like. Everything he was wearing was disheveled.

"What are you doing here?" she asked.

"I heard that there was a murder! Are you alright?"

"You heard so quickly?"

"This is within my jurisdiction."

"Are there other police officers here?"

"Yes, but I told them that I would come talk to you."

"Why?"

"Would you believe me if I said I'm only here because I wanted to make sure that you're okay?"

"Not for a second."

He sighed and sat down. "Just answer the question."

"Just leave."

"No."

She sat up. "What he said is true. I do all of those things he said that I do. I am evil."

"I don't care."

"You are a detective and I am a criminal. Just leave!"

"No."

She stood and slammed her hands onto her desk angrily. "Why are you HERE?"

"I WANT TO *HELP!*"

"Help me with what exactly?"

"I don't care what you do. It doesn't matter anymore."

"You want to go around abduct—"

"No. I don't have to participate in that."

"Why?"

"Because I learned something from you."

"And what's that?"

"There's no use in trying to fix a broken system. I can't stop anyone from committing crimes, so why try?"

"So you're here to be one of us?"

"No. I'm here because I want to be part of something again. There's a void in my life now."

She sighed and sat back down. "Someone broke into my house and killed Annie Elias."

"Why was she here?"

"That's my business."

"I won't tell anyone."

"If you want to be part of this again, tell me the truth."

He sat back in the chair. "What do you want me to tell you?"

"I want to know why you helped me. You aren't stupid. You knew that I was less-than-honest throughout this entire thing. It was not until reality was shoved into your face that you walked away."

"I have been alone my entire life, Jezebel."

"Find a girlfriend."

"I was too miserable to hang on to a woman. Very few reasonably decent looking women are prone to dating someone who is so pathetic."

"And you want what from me?"

"Nothing. I just do not want to be alone again."

"It isn't my job to entertain you."

"I don't want entertainment. I just want company and something to do with my time."

"You're using me."

"You're using me."

She sat back. "Tell me about your childhood."

He laughed. "I don't need you to therapize me, Jezebel."

"Tell me, anyway."

"What do you want to know?"

"Why did you become a police officer?"

"Am I telling a psychologist or a friend?"

"A stranger."

"I wanted to make something of myself without my father's help."

"So, that's what it is all about. A lonely rich boy wanted to prove himself to his father."

"I guess."

"I think that the Elias twins may be my sisters."

Wilson straightened. "What?"

"Someone set me up to hurt my own sisters."

"And then murdered them?"

"Bugsy killed Athena."

"For revenge?"

"She was his niece."

"You cannot be telling me that Bugsy Marcel is your uncle, Jezebel."

"And Michael Saint murdered Annie Elias."

"Did he know?"

"I don't think so, but he's too dead for us to ask him anyway."

The door popped open suddenly, and in came Amir and Hanem. Upon seeing Wilson, Amir's concern melted into irritation.

"What the hell are you doing here?" he asked.

"Close the door," Jezebel said.

"We couldn't find Saint," Hanem said.

"Did you check the restaurant?" Wilson asked.

"No, we didn't," Amir said. "We checked the playground your mother begs for money in."

Wilson's eyes lit up angrily, and he stood. "You arrogant piece of—"

Hanem held him back. "This is not the time."

"He is—"

"Wilson, you are interrupting our productivity and proving yourself to be an obstacle instead of assistance."

"I apologize, Hanem. I'll stop."

"Why did you call him?" Amir asked Jezebel.

"I didn't call him," Jezebel said.

"I cannot believe you brought him here!"

"I already told you that I didn't."

"I can't believe this."

"You need to learn to trust me."

"Because you so often trust me?"

"You don't tell me what to do. I tell *you* what to do."

"Neither of us is five years old."

"You're acting like it."

"I don't want him here."

"I won't keep catering to your feelings."

"Do not make me seem like an overemotional woman."

"There is nothing weak about being a woman."

"Don't put words in my mouth. I didn't say that."

"This is unrelated!" Hanem said. "We have a problem!"

"And what do you suggest?" Jezebel asked.

"We search Quintessence. It's the last link."

"We should have done that already," Amir said.

"It isn't too late," Hanem said.

"But now it will be more difficult. If Saint really killed her, this is more problematic than it was before."

"Jezebel?" Wilson asked.

She stood. "We leave at midnight tomorrow."

"We?" Amir asked.

"Yes, and don't argue."

"You are actually going to come?"

"Yes. Wilson, you can go."

"But—"

"We will see you tomorrow."

He turned and left. Jezebel walked over to her window to watch him go. A minute later, he walked out of the front door, got in his car, and drove away. A moment later, she opened her desk drawer and took out her wallet and keys.

"Where are you going?" Hanem asked.

"Let's go," she said and walked out of the room.

TWENTY-ONE

Hanem and Amir immediately followed her out of the room and down the stairs. Without looking to check if anyone was left in the house, Jezebel went out to her car and threw herself into the driver's seat. Amir opened the passenger door, but he didn't get in with her.

"Do you want me to drive?" Amir asked.

She didn't answer. She just put the key in the ignition and turned it on. Hanem got into the back and Amir took the seat next to her. She pulled out of the driveway and took off down the street.

Try as they might, neither man could convince her to talk to them. She just kept her eyes on the road, focusing on nothing but making it to her destination. Though she hadn't taken this trip in years, she didn't need directions. There was no power on earth that could make her forget. She had tried so many times.

The sun was setting, and the streets were empty. She took highways and bridges west of New York, leaving city lights behind. She had no idea how quickly she was going and didn't think to look for police officers that could stop the car. Reality no longer meant anything to her, and consequences ceased to exist.

The scenery gradually began to change. The further she went, the more rural the roads became. Highways were a thing of the past as she shot down streets that tore through deserted land. Empty open space spread for miles on either side of the car. Every so often, they passed a gas station or small house, but no one seemed to be inside. The only sign of life was the sound of a pack of coyotes howling in the distance.

Street lamps with feeble lights had been posted sparingly in clusters, but all that pierced the darkness were the car's headlights. If anything lay ahead of them, they wouldn't be able to see it until they were too close to stop. This didn't deter her or slow her down. Her foot seemed to have fallen asleep on the gas, the brake pad's existence forgotten.

Hours passed, and she didn't stop. No one asked for a break. No one asked her to pull over. They just barreled along with her, confused but quiet.

The sun began to rise, and heat settled in. Amir rolled down his window, and the sound of the wind cut through the silence. Her hair flew in different directions, but she didn't react. He closed it and moved the loose strands away from her face.

Natural light finally lit up the area, and they could see what was ahead. Without warning, Jezebel made a hard right off the road and shot through the uncharted area. Amir's head hit the window, and Hanem fell over onto the floor.

"Ouch! Jezebel!" Amir said.

She didn't answer.

"Maybe it would be smart to stop for just a minute," Hanem said.

"No," she said.

They gave up. Ten minutes later, they saw a small house in the distance. It dawned on Amir exactly where they were going.

"This isn't a good idea," he said.

She ignored him and picked up speed. She had reached break-neck speed now, getting steadily more reckless the closer they came to the house.

"Jezebel!" Amir yelled.

"We're going to crash!" Hanem yelled.

She slammed on the brakes, and the car managed to stop just inches from the metal gate in front of the house. All of their seat belts locked, saving them from getting hurt again.

Jezebel turned off the engine, but no one moved. They were all breathing hard, trying to slow their heart rates. After a few moments' rest, she unbuckled her seatbelt and stepped out of the car. The other two followed suit.

They went around the front of the car. Her hand rested gently on the gate, but she didn't open it. Before them was a small, two story house that sat on nothing but dust. There was no front or back yard, and no cars were anywhere in sight. The rusting, metal gate circled the house. It was meant to cut off intruders from all sides, but it was broken in several areas, and the door was barely hanging on its hinges. It had once been difficult to get through, but now it was useless.

"Why are we here, Jezebel?" Hanem asked.

"Because it's time," she said.

Jezebel pushed the gate forward and walked up to the front door. She took a deep breath and knocked. She stepped back, and a few seconds later, the door opened. A man she hadn't seen in ten years stood in front of her.

Age had taken its toll on him. His skin was loose, and there were black dots on his face. He was thin, as if he hadn't ate a full meal in years. He had once been even bigger and stronger than Amir, but he had become so frail that he was leaning on a cane almost completely to hold himself up. When he recognized her, his face melted into a smile.

"Jezebel," he said.

"Adam," she said.

He looked behind her. "I never thought Amir would ever willingly come back here."

"I go where she goes," Amir said.

He stepped aside. "Please, come in."

They stepped in and found themselves in a small living room. It was clean, but the furniture was old and worn. A chipped wooden rocking chair was in the corner and a black cat was asleep on it. The television was on, but the volume was down, and the picture was distorted. She and Hanem sat on the couch, but Amir didn't take more than two steps into the house.

"I've been expecting you," Adam said.

"I know," she said.

"Is there anything you need?"

"Do you still have records of everyone who was here when I was?"

"Too many women passed through here for me to record their names."

"I didn't mean the women."

He sighed and got up. He left the room, and Jezebel sat back. She leaned her head against the back of the couch and watched the wooden ceiling fan's blades turn slowly. She took her sweater off and set it next to her. The house was hot, and this fan was no help at all.

Adam came back in and handed her a thick leather-bound book. It was covered in dust, and the thin paper inside had yellowed. Amir walked over to read over her shoulder. She wiped the leather and opened it. She turned the pages to find the year she had first been brought here. She read through the list until she found the name she had been looking for: Darius White.

She looked up at Adam, "Darius White?" he asked.

"Did you know?"

"I wasn't sure, but I suspected."

She closed the book and gave it back to him. He took it and put it on the table. He walked out and came back with a glass of water. He gave it to her, but she didn't drink it. She just looked at it, trying to prolong the moment of silence.

"Is she upstairs?" she asked.

"Yes, she is."

Jezebel finished the water in one gulp and handed him the glass. He motioned for her to go up the stairs but stopped Amir and Hanem from following her. She hesitantly ascended the staircase on her own. Her chest felt tight, and she was finding it hard to breathe. The loose banister swung back and forth, and each step creaked loudly under her feet.

She finally reached the top and went to the first door on her right. She closed her eyes and rested her forehead on it. It was strangely cold. It felt good against her warm skin. She stood there for a few seconds, trying to pull herself together. Then, she raised her hand and knocked gently.

A faint voice said, "Come in."

Jezebel went inside and shut the door behind her. She looked around. The room was very simple. There was nothing there but a bed and a dresser. The small window was closed, and a dark curtain was pulled over it, keeping out all sunlight. It was hotter in here than it had been downstairs. There was a small fan in the corner, but it was producing only hot air.

She turned her attention to the queen-sized bed, where an old woman lay under three thick blankets. She was too weak to move or get up without help. Her face was pale, and her once golden brown hair had thinned and grayed. Her soft skin had wrinkled, and there were lines all over her face. She had lost so much weight that she was drowning in the little night gown she was wearing. She looked terrible. It was painful to see her that way.

The woman smiled faintly and waved Jezebel over. She motioned for her to sit down on the bed next to her, her hands shaking. Jezebel sat down, and the woman took her hand gently. They held each other's gaze quietly for a few moments, and Jezebel blinked away the tears threatening to form in her eyes.

The woman laughed. "Do I look that bad?"

"I'm sorry, Jane."

"You have nothing to be sorry for."

"I wanted to come."

"You are who I taught you to be."

"Are you dying?"

Jane patted her hand. "Death will catch up to all of us one day."

"That's not what you taught me."

Jane laughed again. "You just don't worry yourself. I'll close my eyes for a bit, and then you can tell me more."

"More about what?" Jezebel asked.

She didn't answer. She leaned her head back and closed her eyes. Once upon, this woman wouldn't have trusted a soul enough to close her eyes in their presence. A second's inattention could be fatal. It was the first lesson Jezebel had ever learned from her, and she never forgot it.

A tall, breathtakingly beautiful woman walked into the empty room a teenaged girl was sitting in. All other women had been dragged out hours before. This one was the only one left, and she had been mentally preparing herself for her turn. The woman sat in the only chair in the room. She motioned to the two brutes who had accompanied her close to leave. Both left without argument and slammed the door shut behind them.

"Hello," the woman said.

The girl said nothing.

"I've heard a great deal about you, love."

The girl's expression didn't soften, and she didn't break her silence.

"They told me that you are the only one they couldn't manage to break. You haven't screamed, or cried, or even tried to escape."

Still, the girl did not respond.

"You must be very damaged."

"I am not damaged," the girl snapped.

The woman sat back in her chair. "Alright then. I will start over. Hello, my name is Jane."

"But is it?"

The woman laughed. It was the first laugh the girl had heard here that hadn't been maniacal or mirthless. There was a confidence about this woman that the girl could not understand. This was no place for a woman to safely roam free, and yet here she was commanding men without even speaking.

"They didn't tell me you were smart."

"What do you want?" the girl asked.

The woman stood and went to the door. She bolted it closed and put the chair under the doorknob. Then, she turned and motioned for the girl to stand up. When she resisted, the woman grabbed her hand and pulled her to her feet. She fixed the girl's clothes and handed her a thick sweater. Someone tried the handle from outside, but it didn't budge. He knocked thunderously on the door from the other side, but the woman ignored it.

"Wear it," the woman said.

"What are you doing?"

"Take that off and put the sweater on."

The girl pulled her ripped blouse off of her body and donned the sweater she had been given. The woman wiped dirt off of the girl's face and walked to the door. She unbolted it and moved the chair, and then pushed the girl into the hall ahead of her. A man who looked taller than the doorway was standing in the hall, and another was angrily walking away in the opposite direction. The man who had been waiting looked familiar. She had seen him before, but he had never touched her.

"Let's go, Amir," the woman said to him, and he followed them down a hallway she had only seen from the floor. It seemed less ominous when trekking through it on her feet, rather than being dragged on her back.

They turned the corner and stopped in front of another metal door. The man she had brought with them pushed it open, but none of them entered. Inside was the same horrific scene she had witnessed many times before.

Six women were in chains on the floor. Two of them had already bled out and lay lifeless with their eyes closed. The same small monstrosity that had tried her patience before had settled it's clawed feet into a girl of about fifteen. She was gagged with a thick piece of rope, keeping her from being able to scream. Her eyes were as wide as they could be, and she was shaking violently.

The creature dug a talon into her chest and dragged it slowly across her body. Blood gushed from it in waterfalls, and it caught every drop as it continued to enlarge the wound. Before it reached her stomach, it let go. It looked at the group of spectators standing in the doorway and inched slowly toward the girl, but the woman blocked its path. She pointed to a fourth warm body in the room. Something akin to agitation fell across its face, but it gave up and turned on its next victim. The woman stepped away and looked at the girl she had brought.

"Would you rather be like them or come and listen

to me?" the woman asked her.

The girl hesitated. "Can I save any of them?"

"Not with my help, but you can save yourself."

The woman's hand clasped around Jezebel's again. Her breathing had become less regulated, and her eyeballs were moving quickly behind closed lids. Sounds started coming from her nose and throat, but Jezebel didn't move or call out for help. It didn't seem right to do anything. She just held her hand tighter and watched.

"What is your real name, Jane?" Jezebel asked.

Between the stifled noises, the woman managed to say, "Adeline."

Her breathing slowed, and the noises stopped. Her hold on Jezebel's hand loosened. Her head fell limply to the side, and a trickle of blood fell from her nose. Time seemed to stop. Nothing existed outside of the bubble that held these two women. Two bodies remained, but only one soul was left. Something incredible had disappeared from the world now, and it would never come back.

"Goodbye, Adeline," Jezebel said.

The door opened, and Adam came in. There was no shock on his face. All that was left was sadness. Jezebel stood and left him in the room alone. She went down the stairs and found Amir and Hanem sitting on the couch. They stopped whispering and looked at her, but she didn't spare them a look. She just opened the front door and stepped outside. They followed her out and shut the door behind them.

"Are we going back?" Hanem asked.

She nodded.

"Can I drive?" Amir asked.

She handed him the keys and walked over to the car. She took the passenger seat, and Amir sat behind the wheel. Hanem retook his spot in the back. After a few seconds of stillness, Amir turned on the ignition and pulled out. He didn't need her to tell him where to go. She closed her eyes and leaned against the window. She fell asleep.

She didn't awaken until there was about an hour left in the drive. Neither man said anything, but Amir handed her a bottle of water. She took a drink, and then remained stoically in her seat for the remainder of the ride.

When they pulled into the drive, Hanem vacated the car and left them alone.

"We can talk about it now," she said.

"Maybe now isn't the best time."

"Just ask."

"Is it mine?"

"Yes."

"No one else has touched you?"

"No."

"I don't want you to come with us tonight, Jezebel."

"I have to."

"You're in a fragile state."

"I am not a weak little—"

"It's different, now. I should have a say in this."

"You do not have a say in what I do."

"That doesn't apply until after you give birth."

"I haven't even decided to keep it yet."

His eyes widened. "You want to get rid of it?"

"I'm not fit to be a mother."

"Were you going to make that decision without at least talking to me about it first?"

"It's my body, not yours."

"I still deserve to know."

"You can't possibly think that I would make a good mother."

It looked like there was something he wanted to say

but couldn't. She nudged him.

"Just say what you want to say, Amir."

"Why won't you admit that the real reason you don't want it is so you won't be tied to me?"

She shook her head. "Why do you always assume that I do things because I don't care about you?"

"That's how you act."

"Why do you want this baby so badly?"

"I'm its father."

"That isn't a good reason."

"I am not asking for us to be a couple or a family. I never have."

"I already made a commitment to you."

"You were just placating me, Jezebel. I know you better than to believe you did that because you wanted to."

"Why do you want this thing, Amir?"

"I just want her."

"You don't know that it's a girl."

"I hope it is."

"I would think you'd rather have a son."

"Because I would want to pass on the overprotective jealousy that makes you want to kill me?"

"So you're aware of how annoying you are."

"Yes, but it isn't wrong."

"I can take care of myself."

"I disagree."

"Why a girl?"

"You won't like my answer."

"Tell me."

He sighed. "So I can protect her better than I did her mother."

"Bringing a baby girl into the world we live in will be dangerous, no matter how hard you try to protect her."

"As long as the child doesn't inherit the bitchy stubbornness of her mother, it will be just fine."

A small laugh escaped her, but she didn't comment. She hadn't decided anything, just yet. He stepped out and went around the car to her door. He opened it and pulled her out.

"What are you doing?" she asked.

He put his arms around her. "Jezebel White, if you get rid our baby, I am going to quit."

She held back a smile. "Don't threaten me."

"And I'll hate you for the rest of my life."

"That isn't too big a jump from where we are right now."

"And I'll tell all your secrets."

"You wouldn't dare."

"And I'll make sure you end up in jail."

"All empty threats."

"You don't want to test that theory."

"I won't be a good mother, Amir."

"You won't know until you try."

"That's a terrible philosophy."

"I don't care."

"What if it's a boy?"

"Bite your tongue."

She pulled away. "We leave in a few hours. Go rest."

"Will you at least stay behind me?"

She didn't answer. She closed the car door and went into the house, leaving him in the driveway alone. There was no answer to that question. That night would be unpredictable.

TWENTY-TWO

Despite the lateness of the hour, the street outside of the restaurant was busy. The only available sources of light were the headlights of cars that rushed past. The moon was barely visible behind the clouds above them, and the air was no colder than was expected for October. There would be no intrusive rain tonight. The only possible obstacles would be what lay inside the building itself.

The structure was three stories high, the first two levels part of the restaurant itself and the third closed off for functions for the choice few who could afford it. It had been built with beautiful red bricks, but the walls of the second and third floors were entirely made up of glass windows. Patrons would be able to look out and gaze over the patio in the back or the wide stretch of land in the front. It rested on two acres, the building taking up just over half of the space, and the rest being used as scenery.

Presently, they stood by the back door of the building. Hanem had dealt with the matter of security cameras, and Wilson had constructed some kind of key by examining the lock itself. Amir stood behind her in the dark, holding a flashlight silently.

Wilson gently pushed the key into the lock and opened the door. They all stepped inside, but she hesitated. It was too easy. One simple lock did not seem sufficient for this kind of business. The door should have had at least two, if not three or four. They all turned to look at her, but she shook her head and stepped in after them, shutting the door behind her.

"Amir, Adel, second floor," she said. "Hanem and Wilson, first."

"And you?" Hanem asked.

"I will take care of the third floor."

"Not alone," Amir said.

"Don't snap at me."

"I am not going to leave you unprotected."

"There are only five of us."

"Then we will all search this floor together," Hanem said.

"Fine. Let's go."

She went to the stairs, and after a few seconds of whispering, they followed her. The steps were made of the same laminate wood as the rest of the restaurant's floor. She walked up the four staircases without looking to see who had come all the way up with her.

They reached the top of the stairs and looked around. The room was completely empty. They walked around, but there was nothing to search. It was simply open space. Jezebel kept her flashlight trained on the floor, looking for any irregularities.

"Nothing," Amir said.

"It was a waste of time, coming up here."

"Let's go back downstairs."

Instead of heading to the second floor to check on the others, they went to search the bottom level on their own. They began with the main dining area, and five minutes later, the rest of their company joined them, also having had no luck at all. They moved around the area in silence, looking under tables and examining the walls, but found nothing.

"We will go to Saint's office," Jezebel said. "Hanem, Adel, and Wilson, go in the kitchen."

Amir walked toward the room in the furthermost left corner at the back of the building, and she followed. It was as empty and undecorated as she remembered, but this time, even the desk was bare. Not a paper or a pen could be found atop it. It was as if someone had emptied the entire office out.

There was, however, one major difference between her first visit and this one: Michael Saint's corpse lay in a bundle on the floor, only one small bullet hole visible in his head.

Both stared at the body in silence for several seconds, trying to comprehend what they were seeing.

"HANEM!" Jezebel yelled.

A moment later, the other three men in their company walked in quickly. They stopped and stared at the body at their feet. His eyes were open, and blood had leaked from the wound down his nose, only to free-fall from the edge of his chin, down his neck, and onto the floor. He couldn't have been dead for very long. Hanem and Wilson sank to their knees and examined the body, both prodding different areas to find additional wounds.

"The blood is still fresh," Wilson said.

"He has been dead for no more than a few hours, if that," Hanem said.

"I thought you said you checked the restaurant," Wilson said to Amir.

"He wasn't here when we checked," Amir said.

"Or maybe you didn't look properly."

"Or maybe I can hit you so hard that you lose your eyesight all together and can no longer look."

"Did you finish with the kitchen, Hanem?" Jezebel asked.

"Not yet. It was larger than I thought."

"Then go."

"You are just going to leave the body here? This is the man who murdered your sister, Jezebel."

"So did I. Back to work."

He walked out of the room, taking Adel and Wilson with him.

"Jezebel," Amir said.

"Not now."

He sighed. "I'll stop acting like I am special. I'm sorry that I tested my boundaries, before."

He turned away and continued to search the floor. She watched him silently, trying to make a decision on what to do next. Amir had a knack for throwing her off course at the most inappropriate times and places.

"Amir."

He didn't turn. "Yes?"

"I'm keeping it."

He straightened and looked at her.

"Really?"

"Yes."

"Why?"

"Because you asked me to."

"Okay."

They both returned to their search, not at all perturbed by the dead body amongst them. It was as if he wasn't even there.

A few minutes later, he said, "I found something!"

He moved the file cabinet and fell to his knees. He rolled the carpet away from the wall, revealing a trapdoor. He pulled it open, and there beneath them was a metal ladder leading down into darkness.

She jerked her head toward the door, and Amir left the room. He quickly returned with the other three in tow. All of them stopped at the edge of the circle and peered into the depths of the darkness. No one made a move to climb down. They all looked at her and waited patiently.

Jezebel gently covered the hole and led them out of the room. Amir shut the door and leaned against it.

"We have to go down," she said. "There is no way around that."

"You're going to come with us?" Amir asked.

"Yes."

"It isn't safe!"

"That does not matter anymore."

"Yes, it does."

"Stop."

"I don't want you in harm's way."

"Well, it's too late for that, isn't it?"

"Just please listen to me."

She ignored him. "Hanem, you and Adel will not come down with us."

"Why?" he asked.

"Because if we are murdered, the person behind this will not get away with it. I expect you to plan this, and Adel to execute."

"You're actively putting your own life in danger," Hanem said. "Have you considered that?

"Yes, I have."

"I've never known you to do that."

"This isn't bravery. It's fate."

"It doesn't have to be," Wilson said.

"Are you coming or not, Wilson?"

"Can't quit now."

They returned to the office, and Amir opened the trap door once more. She stood for several minutes, just looking at the hole.

"Into the valley of death," she said.

"Rode the six hundred," Wilson said.

Amir slowly descended the ladder. Jezebel waited only a few seconds before following him, Wilson close behind her.

As soon as her entire body had gone below ground, she felt the temperature drop drastically and a wave of chills went through her. The warmth of the building did not follow her down the hole. It felt as though she had stepped into a freezer on a hot summer's day. She made her way down the stairs blindly, and moments later, her right foot met the floor. She backed away to allow Wilson to reach the bottom, and then turned to find Amir, realizing that she had accidentally left her flashlight in Saint's office. Amir and Wilson turned theirs on, and her eyes adjusted to the dim light.

They had fallen into a wide hallway entirely made of up of large, gray stones. There was water in the deep cracks in the uneven floor. The hall stretched further than the light could see, leaving them in uncertain territory. There was a faint sound of dripping water, but no pipes were anywhere in sight.

Amir took the lead, and they slowly walked through the darkness, treading softly and trying to make as little noise as possible. The faint dripping grew louder, increasing the menacing touch that hung in the stale air. It was getting more difficult to breathe as they walked on, the area around them so musty that her lungs were forced to work harder to keep her from fainting.

Then suddenly, there was nowhere else to go. The hallway ended, leaving them in front of an empty stretch of wall. They exchanged looks and then felt around for something that could trigger a movement of some kind. After several minutes of fruitless searching, Wilson and Amir turned to Jezebel.

"Should we go back?" Wilson asked her.

"No. Keep looking."

"There isn't anything here," Amir said.

"There has to be. Keep trying."

Amir pushed the wall forward with all his strength, but nothing moved. It wasn't a false barrier. It was just a wall.

Jezebel turned to her right and ran her fingers over the stones. She finally found one that was far less fissured than the rest. She carefully pushed it forward, and the ground began to shake slightly as the wall started to move. The noise this action made resounded loudly off the walls. She covered her ears to lessen the impact of the noise, but the sound cut through her hands and pierced her ears.

This wall revealed yet another hallway, but this one was not empty. At the very end was a thick metal door that was lit up by torches perched on either side. Along the walls were other smaller doors. All were closed and bolted tightly from the outside. Broken glass, metal, pieces of wood and other miscellaneous pieces of trash were littered everywhere, covering almost every inch of the floor. She stepped forward, and instead of meeting a flat surface, her foot set onto an unsteady pile of wood. It shook slightly when she placed her weight onto it, but nothing broke. Amir, however, broke through several piles upon immediate contact, making crashing noises echo through the hall.

It was completely silent now. The sound of water had disappeared and was replaced by whispers. Faint voices hid behind each door on either side of them. A few of them were laughing and giggling, but others were crying out in pain. The voices were unintelligible, but together they were a bone-chilling mixture of paradoxical sound, both delighted and wretched depending on the ears of the listener.

They started moving forward slowly, making their way to the bolted door at the end of the hall. Jezebel kept her gaze from falling on either side of her, feeling her heart pounding in the back of her throat. She was taking deep, irregular breaths and forcing herself to ignore what she couldn't see.

When they reached their final destination, Jezebel put her hand on the cold knob. She turned it slowly, and just as she was about to push it forward, every other door around them popped open. All cheerful sound faded. All that could be heard was screaming and a far-off sound of approaching footsteps. They turned to look around, and the door behind them opened.

She turned and found two large men barreling toward them. Instead of turning to leave, both Amir and Wilson lunged at them. She attempted to help, but Amir blocked her every attempt to join the fight. His fists connected with his attacker's jaw on either side of his face, and the man stumbled back several steps. Amir stepped toward him, but the man lunged forward, pushing him to the ground. Jezebel tried to pull him off, but all she succeeded in doing was causing him to turn on her. He jumped up and threw a punch toward the right side of her face, but she dodged it. Amir reached up and hit him in the back of the skull with a block of wood. The man immediately lost consciousness and toppled to the floor. She turned to find that Wilson had managed to do the same with the other attacker.

Before a moment's breath could be taken, three more burst through another door. Amir and Wilson simultaneously pushed her behind them. Their combined force was too strong for her to keep from stumbling back and falling over.

Two of the attackers engaged in the struggle with Amir and Wilson, but the third went after her. Amir attempted to protect her, but she was too far away. She crawled away from her attacker on her back. Just as he made a grab at her feet, she jumped up and ran down the hall. He didn't hesitate for a moment before taking off after her. His burly build hindered the swiftness of his movement, and she put a substantial distance between them. She ran through a door on her right and closed it quickly, managing to move the deadbolt before he began to ram into it. He made very little impact but refused to give up.

Jezebel turned to look around the room. Instead of seeing something that could be a useful weapon, she found herself surrounded by many, many lifeless bodies. People of different ages and genders lay in piles around her. Many of them seemed fresh enough that their blood had not yet dried completely. Three women lay in a pile, limbs bruised, and clothes torn. The one on the bottom had clearly been dead longer than the other two. She had broken her right arm and looked as though her neck had been snapped. Her throat had deep bruises all around it, and her neck was twisted.

At Jezebel's feet was a little girl who looked no older than eleven. It looked like her neck had also been snapped, and her mouth was hanging wide open. Her nose and several teeth were broken, a few of them having fallen to the floor. She was turned on her side, and her skin was hanging off several parts of her body loosely. Both of her thumbs were broken, as well as her right index finger. All of her wounds were incrusted with a deep burgundy color.

The room was somewhat narrow, forcing bodies to be in close proximity to each other. However, it stretched forward into a darkness she could not see beyond. There were torches hung up on the walls. She took one and began to move further into the dark, carefully stepping around decaying bodies and limbs.

It was more of a crypt than anything else. As she walked, the distinct smell of something akin to gasoline mixed with the repulsive aroma of death and decay filled her nostrils. It was unsettling. Most of the bodies seemed to have been there for a long time. She covered her face with her sleeve to keep her nose safe from the poison and protect her stomach from lurching.

The cracked, gray stone walls were covered in symbols she could not recognize. They were smeared in a liquid that she refused to accept as blood. A few of them looked devilish, in a way. It was like attempting to read a language with unrecognizable characters. On the wall to her right, between small shapes and what she assumed were letters, was a large pair of eyes. It was more vibrant than the rest. It was almost bursting from its canvas to attack the eyes of the beholder.

There were symbols all over the floor as well. However, the plethora of bodies allowed only small bits of them to show. It was all the same cluster of word vomit that tainted the walls, but the floor seemed older. Someone had run out of space on the floor and then moved on to the blank space around him.

She looked up at the ceiling and nearly jumped. Above her was a face that took up a large portion of the ceiling. It was impossible to discern its identity or even the gender. It was essentially just a depiction of a human skull. However, it had very bright, very red, eyes in its sockets. Though it was a dark and unsettling piece, the artist was clearly very talented.

The door popped open somewhere far behind her. The sudden sound made her turn too quickly to stay balanced, and she dropped the torch onto a pile of corpses directly in front of her. They immediately went up in flames, blocking her path to the door. Beyond the fire, she heard both Amir and Wilson calling out faintly. She attempted to shout back, but her voice was lost in the blaze. The fire caught onto other piles of lost lives and quickly grew into an angry incandescent inferno. Thick, black smoke emanated from it. It filled her lungs and forced her into fits of heavy coughs, keeping her from breathing regularly.

Moments later, the fire danced high enough to heat the ceiling. The paint above her began to melt slowly, and it started falling like rain. The paint touched the stone floor she sat on, and she braced herself for the unidentified liquid that would soak her, but it didn't. She waited a few moments before opening her eyes and looking down. She jumped at the sight of what had formed on the floor. Directly staring up at her were intense, angry eyes. They were partially open slits that covered half of its irises. It was an expression of extreme malice. Other symbols lay on either side of her and behind her, but she didn't look at them.

She backed away, but a moment later someone grabbed her arm from behind. She managed to wrench herself free and turned. Another heavyset man had found his way to her. She tried to run, but he caught hold of her shirt. Before he could drag her away, she caught sight of an arm that had caught fire. She grabbed it by its unlit fingers and flung it behind her. She missed the shot by a pathetically wide margin, but he was startled enough to he let her go.

She grabbed another arm and ran behind him, forcing to back up closely to the fire. She swung the arm, and he dove to the right. Before she could swing again, he lunged at her legs, dragging her to the floor and causing the arm she was holding to fall out of her hands. He pulled her up by her hair and began to pull her back toward the dark, but she stopped supporting herself, allowing her body to go limp. The sudden increase in weight made him stop for just a moment, and she took the opportunity to turn on her stomach, reach up, and bite his leg as hard as she possibly could. He released her and she caught hold of his left foot. She pulled it toward her forcefully, and he fell onto his back. She stood quickly and dragged him in the direction of the fire.

However, he was far too strong for her to get very far. As he began to stand, she let go of him and ran as close to the fire as she possibly could without burning any part of her. He ran toward her, and just before he reached her, she fell flatly onto the floor. He tripped over her body and fell forward. She rolled away from the fire and stood to see the damage. His entire body—ankles to skull—was engulfed in flames. She watched him slowly burn to death. She took no sick pleasure in watching it happen, but she needed confirmation that he was no longer a threat.

She sat in front of the fire, cross-legged, head in hands. She was gasping heavily, trying to breathe through her sleeve to avoid inhaling the smoke. She could no longer see Amir or Wilson, and the fire was still growing. She took to her feet once more and backed away toward the dark again. She hadn't gone more than ten feet before something heavy connected with the back of her head. Her head spun, and then her entire world went black.

Some time later, her eyes opened, and she found herself in a circular room with other unconscious people. She had been laid between Wilson and Amir, who had not yet opened their eyes. She was relieved to see that both were still breathing, but Amir had been tied with so much rope and twine that it dug into his skin. He was bleeding. Wilson was only handcuffed and forced to the floor.

She observed the others around her and was shocked to find a lifeless Jules at her feet. His mouth was open, and his tongue seemed to have been bitten off. There were several bullet wounds in his chest and one in his forehead. Though his skin was naturally dark in color, he seemed faint. His eyes were closed, and his right arm was bent in a position that suggested it was broken. She was the only one who was not bound, and she recognized no one else.

Just as she began to stand, she felt something rest against the back of her skull. It was some kind of firearm, and whoever wielded it grabbed hold of her arm. He turned her slowly, not lowering the gun or allowing it to rest anywhere other than her head. His face was covered with a black balaclava, and she could see nothing of him but his brown eyes. They were extremely familiar—as if she had stared into them for years. He slowly reached up and peeled off the mask.

Her blood ran cold. This was the second time she had been brought face to face with him without warning, but she wasn't surprised; disgusted and angry, but not surprised. He had been haunting her for months.

"Dad."

"Little girl."

TWENTY-THREE

"You don't look surprised," he said.

"I'm not, but I don't understand."

"What don't you understand?"

"You were dead. I saw your body," she said. "You were dead and bleeding on the floor, miles away from here."

"You saw what you wanted to see."

She took a step back and crossed her arms. "Psychological warfare no longer works on me. Tell me the truth."

He laughed. "A few well-aimed bullets to the chest and you assumed that I was murdered? You should know better than that, Jezebel."

"No one is that good an actor."

"I didn't have to be. You ran off so quickly. So afraid to see me dead, weren't you?"

"I was happy you were dead."

"That isn't a very smart thing to say right now."

"Why did you do this to me?"

He didn't answer. Instead, he looked to Wilson and Amir and kicked them roughly. Their eyes opened, and

Amir jumped when he noticed who was there. Wilson rolled over, looking dazed and confused. Both tried to stand, but they were bound so tightly that they fell over again.

"Let me go!" they yelled together.

"No," her father said lightly.

"Who are you?" Wilson asked.

"I owe you no answers."

"LET ME GO!" Amir yelled again.

Her father ignored him and turned his attention to her once more. "You came yourself."

"How did you know that I would?"

"I didn't. I hoped."

"You told me that hope is a consolation for the weak."

"And I was right."

"You are about to murder your only daughter."

"You aren't."

"Excuse me?"

"You are not my daughter."

"Then what do you want with me?"

"You are the reason your mother is dead."

"But you are the reason she lost her mind. Do not blame me for what you've done to her."

"It's all the same."

"Why did you leave her, if she matters this much to you?"

"Your mother is a lying slag."

"Watch what you say about my mother."

"You want me to reveal my master plan?"

"This isn't a movie."

"Then why am I enjoying it so much?"

"Stop playing with me."

"You are not my daughter. You are the bastard daughter of the late Dixon Shepherd."

"Excuse me?" Wilson asked.

"Yes, Asher. This atrocity is your sister."

"That isn't possible."

"But it is. Her mother was a prostitute."

"THAT ISN'T TRUE!" Jezebel yelled.

"I couldn't believe it either, Jezebel," her father said. "You see, many years ago, your mother met Dixon Shepherd, a selfish adulterous millionaire. It was all she had ever wanted in life; money, diamonds, status."

"But she was already dating you."

"Married. She had married me. She had been planning to leave me, but when Shepherd found out about her pregnancy with you, he turned on her and told her to get rid of the baby. He was also married, you see."

"And she pretended I was your daughter."

"Yes, and then her mother got sick, and I sent her off to Greece. She refused to leave your brother with me. She couldn't trust me to take care of Lionel. He was not my son."

"And she had Athena and Annie."

"That she did."

"You murdered Lionel."

"I did no such thing. I paid to have him murdered."

"Are you Hadley Scott?"

"We've all got our non de plumes."

"You're picking off my mother's children, one by one."

"You forced me to."

"How could that possibly have been my fault?"

"I had arranged for you to be taken. I didn't tell them that you are my daughter, but you were beautiful enough that no questions were asked. I was so angry that she had lied to me that I wanted to get rid of you."

"And you did."

"But you escaped. You found your way out and even profited from what I had done. Nothing infuriated me more, and I couldn't let you win."

"Why did you wait so long?"

"To torture you."

"I still don't see how all of it comes back to me."

"You escaped. You ruined my revenge. That is what fueled all of this. I wasn't going to hurt anyone but you, and then I changed my mind. I wanted all of her children now."

"You're psychotic."

"Maybe, but had it not been for your brother, I would have never found out that she had cheated on me. I forgave her for Lionel, because I truly loved her. At least she had apologized."

"You're murdering all of her children as revenge for her affairs?"

"Don't say it as if it isn't justified."

"Murder is never justified."

He laughed. "You are one to talk."

"Why was Lanyard after me?"

"He was just after your money, and he wouldn't be able to manage it with you still breathing. He wasn't very bright."

"He had no place in this story."

"He did, actually."

"What's that?"

"If it hadn't been for him, you wouldn't have finally committed a murder by choice."

"My record wasn't clean."

"But your hands were. It was the only way you could live with yourself, not having fired a gun."

"That isn't enough of a reason to involve him."

"I wanted him dead for other things, and what more entertaining a way could there be to get rid of him than to use him to torture you?"

"Why did you kill Bugsy and Saint?"

"They knew too much. I couldn't allow them to continue breathing when they were so great a liability.

Saint was a naïve idiot, and Marcel had done nothing to deserve to live."

"That is not your decision, who deserves what."

"And you have been doing what for the past six years?"

"It isn't the same."

"It is exactly the same."

"Why didn't you just kill me? Why go to all this trouble?"

"Death is a relief that you do not deserve."

"Then what are you going to do to me?"

He smiled widely. "I'm going to make all of your dreams come true."

"What does that mean?"

He smiled and made a motion with his hand. She heard footsteps approaching from all around her. It sounded like an entire army was closing in on her, but it wasn't the sound of human feet. The steps weren't loud enough to belong to a group of men. This was a sound that hadn't rung in her ears in years. She shut her eyes just before they all stepped into the light. She heard Wilson cry out in terror and bowed her head against her chest.

Memories were long gone. Nothing was going to distract her from what was coming. She tried to regulate her breathing and bit so harshly into her lip that warm blood filled her mouth. She gritted her teeth to subdue her building panic, but nothing was working. Her chest tightened, and panic consumed her from navel to nose.

"Open your eyes," he father said.

She ignored him. He walked over and grabbed her face roughly. He dragged her closer to him and whispered, "Open your eyes."

"No," she managed to say.

"Open your eyes!" he yelled.

"No!"

He dug one hand into her hair and tried to force her eyelids open with the other. She turned her face away, but she couldn't avoid him. The harsh impact of his fingers against her face's fragile sockets startled her enough to make her eyes pop open involuntarily.

There they were. She finally saw them again. Hundreds of identical monstrosities had closed in on them, all of them wearing the same malicious expressions and seeming ready to pounce on her.

They appeared to be slightly different than she had remembered. They were tall enough to be at level with her hips, and their eyes were bright red. They seemed to have more muscle under their leather wings, and the slits that had been used for intake of air were wider. The steel traps they had in the place of their mouths were open, revealing rows upon rows of teeth. They now had five sharp talons on each of their small feet, instead of just three.

There was a look of extreme hunger in their eyes. They had been deprived of their form of sustenance for a long time and were close to losing control. They had been forced into chains on their stomachs and around their feet. Each creature's wing was strapped tightly to its body. They were all attached to each other, and a thick metal chain was stuck to each of their backs and was connected to something far off in the dark. Many of them were trying to fight through their bounds.

The hostility that emanated from each of them was terrifying. They were trying to yell out at her, but these had been born without speech. All that they could do was make indiscernible animal noises and try to break free.

Most of them seemed to recognize her. They snarled and tried to go after her, but they couldn't advance another step in any direction. Her father stood behind her and laughed in her ear.

"I'm going to unchain them," he said. "You will all die."

She didn't say anything.

"Unless," he said.

"Stop playing with me," she said.

"I will let two of you go, and I want you to tell me who."

"Excuse me?"

"Tell me who you want me to save. If you'd like to save yourself and sacrifice them, I'm open to that."

"I can't do that."

"Yes, you can."

"You won't take my suggestion."

"On my honor, I will."

"You have no honor."

"You aren't in a position to debate that."

"Why would you let me go?"

"Because forcing you to live with yourself after ordering the death of someone you love will be just as sweet as watching you be torn limb from limb. Either way, I win."

"I can't make that decision."

"But you will."

She turned to the other two men who had come with her. Neither Wilson nor Amir said one word, but the expression on each of their faces clearly expressed that they were sincerely afraid for her more than for themselves, for different reasons. Wilson would lose his last living relative for the second time. Amir would lose his daughter and the woman he had made the mistake of falling in love with, and whom had somehow fallen in love with him in return.

Wilson was yet another family member whose murder she would be responsible for. Everyone who had ever shared a bloodline with her had met a fatal end. She was alone in her world, knowing that everyone who had ever been tied to her would ultimately die too soon.

"I will not hate you for choosing to save yourself, Belle," Amir said.

She couldn't even look at him.

"Listen to me," he said. "You aren't selfish. You're different now."

She looked at Wilson, who said, "I want to live, but I won't pressure your decision. Do what you want. I won't hate you for it."

"Choose, Jezebel," her father said.

A sense of calm suddenly settled in on her. The building panic fell away, and she turned away from all the humans in the room. She walked around the circle and looked at all of them more closely. There were small almost unnoticeable differences between each of them. Some of them had different shades of red eyes, and some were taller than others. A few had spurts of white on their wings, and others were completely black. Even the levels of hostility varied. The angriest of them had red saliva dripping from their open mouths and were breathing so hard their chests were rising and falling at an alarming pace.

Her eyes fell on one in particular that was far more different than the rest. There was something different about it. It wasn't fighting the chains and didn't look as angry as the rest. It hadn't softened, but it was as if its will to fight had disappeared. Its mouth was closed, and it was making no noise. She walked away from her father and stood in front of it. It looked up at her, and its eyes turned from red to a dark gray color. All of what was left of its initial hostility faded.

"What are you doing?" her father asked.

She didn't answer. She walked over to the creature and sat cross-legged in front of it. They locked eyes and held each other's gaze, ignoring the others that were fighting to attack her. It wasn't standing up straight, unlike the others. It was hunched over slightly, its wing hanging limply behind it. It was the only one that had three talons, and it was shorter than the rest. It was so familiar. It was as if she had formed a bond with this one, once upon a time.

She raised her hand and slowly moved toward its head.

"Jezebel," Amir said.

She didn't look his way. The creature followed her hand with its eyes but didn't protest or move. She gently placed it on its head and patted it. The leather-like skin was rough and covered with some kind of clear slime, but she didn't recoil. It closed its eyes, and she felt its muscles relax under her touch. A few seconds later, she let go and moved away.

She looked around her for something sharp and found pieces of shattered glass a few feet to her right. She picked up a shard and dug it into her hand, making a deep cut in the center of her palm. Blood oozed from it, setting the other creatures into a higher energy frenzy, but she didn't notice them.

She lifted her hand to the one in front of her and held it up to its mouth. It looked at her blankly for a few seconds, and then opened it mouth and lapped up the blood in her hand slowly. The saliva from its tongue sent a burning sensation into the open wound, but she didn't react. Its eyes began to change back into red, and the longer is drank, the brighter the color became.

It was as if she had recharged a battery. The thing became as animated and angry as the rest. It shrieked and tried to break out of its binds. The chains were too strong, but it continued trying to attack her. Its blood-tainted saliva sputtered out of its mouth and tainted her face and clothes. She didn't move away or attempt to wipe any of it off. It didn't bother her. She took a deep breath and finally stood up. She turned back to her father.

"Just let them get me," she said.

END

ABOUT THE AUTHOR

Hend Salah is a New York born, horror loving, mental health counseling, loud-mouthed mass of contradictions.

She has a cornucopia of sensibly insensible, controversial opinions, and is allergic to romance. She loves putting a dark twist on a good argument. Bad things are funny. Good things are boring. She sees the world as a dark place, disguised with an artificial candy coating, drugged up with happy pills.

Once upon a Midnight Dreary, she was a journalist. She has written for several news outlets and runs her own website: *Insertprofessionalwebsitetitlehere.com.* There, she shares some of her professional work, somewhat twisted thoughts, and dark humor.

Hend is currently a counselor at Franklin Academy, and spends her days working with kids and writing under cover of darkness.

Other HellBound Books Titles
Available at:
www.hellboundbookspublishing.com

Them

Ray Sanders returns home from Florida to bury his mother.

Soon, the supernatural evidence behind his mother's demise begins to surface in the form of dreams and mysterious happenings.

During all of the madness, Sanders must face his destiny and vanquish the generations-old evil that has plagued his family since the 1800's…

In 1854, Louis Sanders, with the help of Elias Atkins, dug a well to provide water to the family farm. What they did not anticipate was the water to be infested with Odomulites - ancient sins. These malevolent beings - were trapped in our world on their way to the spirit world - formed a pact of protection with both Sanders and Atkins; the families would serve as guardians of the Odomulite nests and in return, a blind eye would be cast when the Odomulites took host bodies to inhabit and feed upon. It was this pact, which in 2016 would propel Sanders and Julie Fontaine - a young woman with a special connection to the Spirit World - into the heart of the last active nest to rid the town of its insidious Odomulite population.

Blood in The Woods

Based upon true events...

For Jody, growing up in the late eighties and early nineties in the small Louisiana town of Hammond with his best friend Jack was filled with wonderful childhood memories.

Time spent playing in the woods, shooting pellet guns, blowing up mailboxes, fighting at school and upon the dawning of interest in the fairer sex, their carefree lives typical of children with few responsibilities and no worries beyond the next pop-quiz or getting to second base. As they grow older together and experience the joys and pains of life, love, family and friendship, they uncover a grim secret that their home town has kept, and through little more than an innocent, idle curiosity, Jody and Jack stumble upon something horrific in the woods and their lives quickly take a most sinister and dangerous turn as they find themselves hunted by an unspeakable evil...

Down by the Sea and Other Tales of Dark Destiny

This exceptional collection follows the inevitable path travelled towards truth or justice, whether their own, or from the universe at large:

A tough teen meets his match in an elderly woman who has been ridding the neighborhood of its thugs, one by one.

A repeat drunk driver is cursed to spend the rest of his days trapped behind the wheel.

A pregnant teen murders her parents and devises a gruesome nativity scene.

A woman uncovers a preacher's deadly solution to ridding the world of evildoers.

A serial killer looks to reunite with his estranged mother, only

The little things you think you see can lead to crippling paranoia, but a little self-surgery can take care of your troublesome eyes.

A young woman discovers her family's fate is to sacrifice themselves to horrific mermaids.

An anxious gardener murders his nosy neighbor to keep the secret about his chemically-enhanced prize rose garden.

A woman is afraid of the dark because it will release the beast that lives inside her.

A woman tries hypnotherapy for childhood trauma and learns her abuser is now her doctor.

A woman tries to forget the murders of her baby and husband by ignoring the proof in the back seat of her car.

Satan seeks revenge on the woman who spurned him by forcing her to give birth to him.

A dying woman returns to her childhood home and encounters the ghosts of her enslaved ancestors.

War Game

The tenants never saw it coming.

The Murray building, constructed in the seventies by the eccentric billionaire Samuel Murray, contains a secret so horrific and abhorrent that those caught up in his nefarious social experiment might never see the light of day again.

Time is ticking.

Only one person can beat the War Game and walk away with a cool $100 million in cash.

Who dies? Who lives? Who is the real villain? What is the building's biggest secret, and why do only a select few know about it?

War Game is a brutal, maniacal thriller with enough plot twists to make your head spin and your stomach churn. There's violence aplenty, murder, mayhem, and buckets of blood…

Can you predict the outcome?

Dead is Dead; But Not Always

A wonderfully eclectic collection of disturbingly good short stories…

The mountain winds howl and blood flows to appease, tradition runs deep and transforms the skin for the sake of togetherness.

Buried beneath the soil is a book to bridge the eternal dark with the light of life.

God's way is with a hiss but Satan's way is with a kiss, and in the Arctic only the bears can hear your screams.

When it's your time go the lake will tell you, and being a kid ain't easy when the natural and supernatural collide to peel the layers from your back.

From dread to thriller to cosmic, the seven novelettes collected here meld into one bone-jarringly bleak outing, bound to rattle cores and test readers' nerves.

Dead is Dead, but Not Always is the first solo collection from Canadian author Eddie Generous.

Demons, Devils and Denizens of Hell: Vol, 2

The second volume in HellBound Books' outstanding horror anthology fair teems with tales of Hades' finest citizens – both resident and vacationing in our earthly realm…

Compiled by the inimitable P. Mattern and featuring: Savannah Morgan, Andrew MacKay, Jaap Boekestein, James H Longmore, Stephanie Kelley, Ryan Woods, James Nichols, P. Mattern, Marcus Mattern, Gerri R Gray, and legion more…

Shopping List 2: Another Horror Anthology

Once again, HellBound Books brings you an outstanding collection of horror, dark, slippery things, and supernatural terror - all from the very best up and coming minds in the genre.

We have given each and every one of our authors the opportunity to have their shopping lists read by you, the most wonderful reading public, and have the darkest corners of their creative psyche laid bare for all to see...

In all, 21 stories to chill the soul, tingle the spine and keep you awake in the cold, murky hours of the night from: Erin Lee, The Truth Artist, John Barackman, Serena Daniels, M.R. Wallace, Isobel Blackthorn, Alex Laybourne, Jason J. Nugent, Josh Darling, Jovan Jones, Nick Swain, Douglas Ford, Craig Bullock, Craig Bullock, Jeff C. Stevenson, PC3, David F Gray, Sergio Palumbo, Donna Maria McCarthy, David Clark & Megan E. Morales

A HellBound Books LLC Publication

http://www.hellboundbookspublishing.com

Printed in the United States of America

www.ingramcontent.com/pod-product-compliance
Lightning Source LLC
Chambersburg PA
CBHW060535190726
48283CB00003B/736